Kathy:
May all your wishes come true!

A
Midnight
Clear

Kim Beall
Dec. 2020

Kim Beall

A Midnight Clear

This is a work of fiction. All characters, places, and events described within are
products of the author's imagination or are used fictitiously.

Except Doctor Boojums. He is absolutely real, and will fight anyone who says
otherwise.

ISBN 978-1-7339964-4-0
Published in the United States of America
Illustrations by Kim Beall

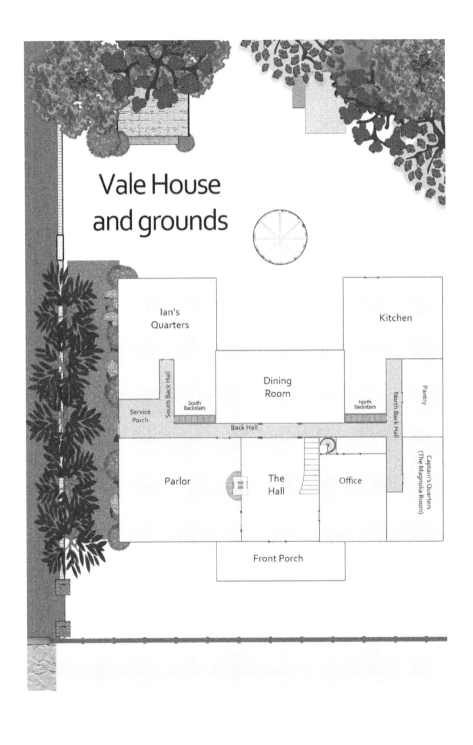

Vale House and grounds

Ian's Quarters

Kitchen

South Back Hall

Dining Room

Pantry

Service Porch

South Backstairs

North Backstairs

North Back Hall

Back Hall

Parlor

The Hall

Office

Captain's Quarters (The Magnolia Room)

Front Porch

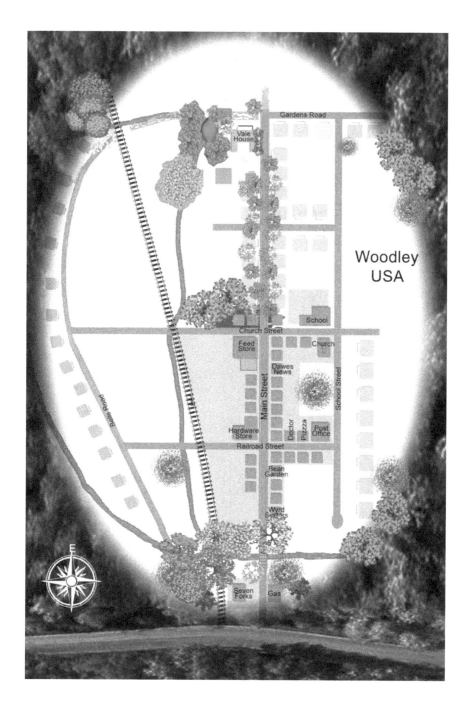

For Gary, whose unconditional support for all
my crazy ideas continues to be my wish come
true, every single day.

Preface

Dear Readers:

This volume of the Woodley, USA story-cycle falls chronologically between Book 2 (*Moonlight and Moss*) and Book 3 (*Ghost of a Chance*.) I wrote it as a Christmas gift for my beloved readers. It is not necessary to have read any of the other stories to enjoy this one, but beware: if you do read this book without having read the others, you might find yourself wanting to know more about Woodley and its quirky denizens. Fortunately, this is an easily remedied dilemma.

Merry and Blessed whatever you are celebrating, and remember: ghosts are people, too!

Kim Beall

Contents

December

21

Winter Solstice

1- Make a Wish

You'd better think about it before he gets here!"

Katarina waved the end of a plastic holly garland at Cally, causing the desk chair on which she was standing to wobble. Cally gasped and ran to steady the chair.

"She's not kidding," said Bethany. The receptionist was arranging a row of white pillar candles along the mantelpiece behind the desk. She had a sprig of the same plastic holly tucked into her long, silver curls. "Santa really doesn't like it if you don't have a wish prepared for him."

Cally shook her head and handed the roll of tape up to Katarina. She had begun to realize Christmas was celebrated a bit differently here in Woodley, USA, particularly at Vale House, and not just because it was famously haunted by more spirits than Santa could pack into his sack.

Still, all the bright ornaments from the boxes Ignacio had brought in from the barn did make the Reception Hall feel festive. Cally had to smile in spite of herself, watching (and trying to find a way to help) Katarina and Bethany layer the decorations on thicker and thicker.

"I get it!" Katarina laughed and climbed down from the chair to admire her handiwork. The wide doorway between the Hall and the dining room was now framed in green leaves with red berries and a tasteful hint of tinsel. "I get it! You don't believe in Santa! Do you?" The short, round woman, a few years younger than Cally, put her hands on her hips and nodded sternly, though her dark eyes still twinkled. "That's alright, you don't have to believe. But you still have to make a wish!"

"Oh..." Cally picked a red glass ornament out of the box on the desk and turned it over in her hands. "I don't mind Santa. I guess

I believe in the spirit of him, anyway. It's just that I don't believe in wishes. Not anymore."

"Callaghan McCarthy!" Bethany was at least fifteen years older than Cally. Her eyes didn't twinkle the way Katarina's did, but her smile was usually just as warm. Except for now, when her lips were drawn into a hard line as she scolded. "How could you even say such a thing? You have everything a woman your age could wish for! Your new book has just come out, and it's selling well." She counted on her fingers as she enumerated Cally's blessings. "Your children are happy and healthy, and you'll get to see them both over the holidays. You have a grandson on the way, and you even have a new romance in your life. With a very handsome gentleman, if I may say so. And on top of it all you live in the best haunted bed and breakfast this side of the interstate!"

Cally had to laugh, then. "You're right. I am a lucky woman. Even though my children's father will be visiting for Christmas, too. I'm sure I'll be able to handle that okay – at least he's staying at the Yellow House with them, not here! But you're wrong about one thing."

Katarina had started to extract a string of tiny white lights from one of the boxes, but she stopped with them still balled up in her hands. "And what is that? You know Bethany's never wrong about anything."

Both Bethany and Katarina laughed so giddily at this, Cally suspected they might have broken into the holiday brandy a few days early. She considered doing the same, maybe, later. Meanwhile, she explained herself. "It's just that this is not the best haunted bed and breakfast this side of the interstate." Quickly, before their laughter could turn into exclamations of outrage, she added, "It's the finest bed and breakfast on either side of any interstate."

The two women laughed again, louder and longer this time, while turning to help one another untangle the lights. Cally considered the red globe in her hands and, making up her mind, nestled it gently into the tinsel garland between two of the candles on the mantel.

The ornament had left red glitter all over her palms. She let out a quiet snort. She hated glitter.

"Oh, well, I suppose I'm going to be up to my eyebrows in it for the next few days," she muttered quietly to herself, reaching back into the box for another glass ball. Out loud, she asked, "So, who plays Santa, anyway? I bet it's Merv Arkwright. He's got the right build for it. Or is it Ian?" She thought Ian May would probably be the best candidate, with his wide, generous smile, but he had lost quite a lot of weight, last time she'd seen him; his Santa suit would need more than a few pillows to fill it out. "Is that why Ian and Sofie are taking time away from their sailing adventures to come home for Christmas?"

"*My* hope is they're coming home to stay," Bethany said bluntly. "I'd make that my wish, this year, except we're not allowed to make wishes that interfere with anyone's free will. Ian and Sofie are both too old to be off sailing, especially this time of year! But as to your guesses: no, and no. Wrong on both counts. Nobody can play Santa, except Santa."

As if in answer, Santa Claus appeared at the top of the grand staircase. At least, a skinny, dark-skinned young man wearing a red hat did. His dimples were indeed merry, though his '*Run, Run Rudolph*' t-shirt was probably not something Santa would have chosen to wear. The jolly apparition called "Ho, Ho, Ho!" down the stairs, but of the three living humans in the Hall, only Cally could hear this. Making sure the other women's attention was elsewhere, she threw him an "I'll talk to you later" wink. He bowed with a flourish and vanished.

Katarina was still bent over the box of lights, her black ponytail bobbing as she struggled with a complicated snarl. At last she straightened, holding up a length of tangle-free wires and little clear bulbs. "Ta-da!"

Bethany applauded.

Katarina's satisfied grin spread even wider as her gaze shifted over Cally's shoulder to the front door.

Cally turned around to see a tall silhouette wavering in the middle of the leaded glass oval. The door was already opening, and Katarina's husband rushed through it, one hand reaching back to stop the screen door slamming behind him.

"And here is just the man to help us hang these up!" Trailing

Christmas lights, Katarina bustled past Cally to stand on tiptoe and kiss Ignacio on the cheek. "I think these should go above the door to the parlor." She pointed with one hand, holding the string of lights out to him with the other.

"I'm afraid I can't help right now," Ignacio said. He took the lights absently into his hands, but he only looked down at Katarina, and then over to Cally. His face was drawn, his eyes wide and serious. "The sheriff is on his way."

"Whatever for?" Bethany looked up from the box she'd been rifling through. "Are we violating some kind of fire code with all these lights?" She laughed at her own joke, though it wasn't far from the truth.

"I'll put the coffee pot on!" Katarina dusted bits of tinsel off her apron and turned toward the kitchen. "Dunn always likes hot coffee on cold days!"

"No." Ignacio stopped her in mid-dash. "He's not going to have time for coffee. Not right now. Luke has found a body in the pond."

The stunned silence that filled the Hall lasted only a second.
"Ian!"

Cally wasn't sure whether it was herself or the other women who had shouted the name, but all three of them hurried past Ignacio to the door.

"It isn't Ian!" Ignacio had to shout to make himself heard above the clamor of all three of them trying to get the door open at once. "It isn't Ian. It's... well, neither of us recognized him. It's a stranger, someone from outside of town."

Cally let out a breath. In a small town like Woodley, if neither Ignacio nor the town pizza-delivery guy recognized the body, then it had to be someone Not From Around Here. That meant it was almost certainly nobody she knew and loved, but it was still a shocking matter.

"What was a stranger doing down by our pond?" Cally wrapped her arms around herself to quell the shudder that crept through her. "Anyway that pond's not deep enough for someone to drown in. Unless..." If there was a body in the pond, she thought, someone had to have put it there. The thought that foul play had been committed so close to the house made her stomach turn over, and not just because she'd been walking outside along the fence last night...

"No, it's probably not anything shady." Ignacio smiled down at her, putting a reassuring hand on her shoulder. "He was trapped under the ice."

Cally didn't feel the least bit reassured by this, but before she could say so she saw more figures outside the door. She opened it once more to see both Sheriff Mahon and Jacob Lucas coming up the porch steps. Once they reached the top, however, they held back, pointing apologetically to their wet boots and pants cuffs.

"Don't be ridiculous," she called out to them. "Get in here before you freeze to death." She winced at her choice of words as she pushed the screen door open.

The sheriff took off his hat and Luke took off his pizza delivery cap. As they shouldered past her into the warm Hall, Katarina nodded to Ignacio.

"See?" she said, resuming her dash to the kitchen. "I'll get the hot coffee!"

2 – A Stranger in Town

I was delivering a double-cheese to the Ridel cottage." Luke had apparently already told his story to the sheriff, who stood waiting patiently while it was repeated for the benefit of the Vale House staff.

"I usually cut through the field behind y'all's property, instead of following Railroad Street, since the Ridels live on the east end of Bells Road. I didn't even notice anything weird until I was headed back. I guess that's a good thing, because Mrs. Ridel doesn't like it if her melted mozzarella cools off!" He started to laugh, but the others didn't join in, so he continued. "It really just looked like a long blob of shadow under the ring of ice around the edge of the pond. I stopped to look closer, then I ran and fetched Ignacio. He managed to drag it out with a rake enough to where we could see it really was a body. That's when Ignacio called the sheriff."

"Well thank you for fetching Ignacio instead of coming to tell us!" Bethany's face was as pale as the candles on the mantelpiece, and she'd had to sit down in the desk chair. "I wouldn't even have been able to dial the phone! The thought of a dead body down there..."

"We've already removed it from the pond." The sheriff accepted a steaming white mug from Katarina, nodding his thanks. "An ambulance is on its way right now from Blackthorn to pick it up. I just thought I'd better let you all know before it gets here. The EMS guys will have to drive across your lawn to get to the pond, and I didn't want you to be alarmed." He sipped deeply from the mug, and a smile of appreciation spread across his face. Katarina always knew just how everyone liked their coffee.

Katarina handed another mug to Luke. "It always takes those

EMS drivers forever to find Woodley," she said. "Good thing whoever it is is already dead...oh! Oh, no, I didn't mean it that way!" She crossed herself quickly, muttering something in Spanish that Cally thought sounded like a little prayer. Ignacio put a comforting arm around her.

"Well, Ms. Chase." Sheriff Mahon turned from Katarina to Bethany. "I'm sorry if this sounds indelicate, but I do have to ask. Were you expecting any new B&B guests this afternoon? On account of the, erm, victim is a stranger to Woodley and all."

Bethany shook her head. "We aren't expecting anyone until after New Year's Day."

Cally added, "My daughter Kelleigh and her husband will be arriving at the Yellow House on the twenty-third. But you and Luke met them at the Captain's funeral, so you'd recognize them. Anyway that's two days from now. Sheriff, didn't you check...you know. The body's wallet, or pockets or anything? Surely he had some kind of ID on him."

Katarina crossed herself again – probably at the thought of someone rifling through a dead man's pockets.

"Of course we did, Ms. McCarthy." Sheriff Mahon nodded. "There was nothing. Well, there was a set of keys. I'm about to head out to the interstate to see if they might fit a car I spotted parked on the shoulder this morning, if it's still there. It did have out-of-state plates."

As he turned back to the door, red and blue lights began flashing in the leaded glass oval in a particularly un-Christmaslike way. Luke and Ignacio started to follow him but he said, "I've got this. You all stay here and carry on as you were. I'll call if I find out anything new." He glanced over his shoulder at Cally, but tilted his head toward Katarina and Bethany. Cally guessed he was really trying to say: *Do me a favor and keep these ladies from watching them carry the body up the hill, would you?"*

Ignacio tightened his arm around Katarina, and Cally laid her hands on Bethany's shoulders in what she hoped seemed more like a gesture of comfort than of restraint. Luke, however, quaffed the rest of his coffee and trailed the sheriff out the door, waving as he went and saying, "Great coffee, as always Kat! I better be getting back to my store – I've left it unattended way too long!"

"I'm sure your loyal customers will understand," Cally told his retreating back. She knew they would understand, because the news had probably already spread all over town. No news ever went unknown for long in Woodley.

In fact, the phone on the desk began to ring before Luke's footsteps had quite faded from the porch. Bethany flew into action, jabbing buttons on the telephone console like the pro she was. "Vale House Bed and Breakfast Bethany speaking will you hold please?" she said all in one breath, pushed a different button and said again, "Vale House Bed and Breakfast Bethany speaking will you hold please?" Between button-pushings, she glanced meaningfully up at Cally. Cally nodded and headed toward the carved door near the base of the stairs, where the phone in her office had already begun to ring with the calls Bethany was transferring.

Cally spent the better part of the next hour at her own desk, then, saying, "Yes, the sheriff knows about it," "No he doesn't know who it was," "Yes the EMS is here (*of course you know that - you watched them come down Main Street yourself,*" but not out loud) and "Thank you. You have a Merry Christmas, too."

While taking one call after another, she glanced up at her computer screen. A single light winked in the upper right corner, telling her she'd received a new message via her antique (as computers go) chat program. "Damn, has Emerald found out about it already, too? Sorry! Sorry, Ms. Harper, I didn't mean to say that out loud. No, Emerald doesn't live in Woodley. She's an old friend of mine from...from before I moved here. Yes, ma'am, I promise to be more careful of my language."

She hung up the phone at last and sat back, relishing the relative silence, and the fact that the flashing red and blue lights outside the window had finally gone away. Out in the Hall, she could hear Bethany chatting animatedly with the last caller.

"Oh, I know!" She was laughing, so Cally knew she must have got over the shock by now. "I know, right? Everybody knows you don't go walking across the ice on any pond in the South! I mean we hardly ever get ice this early in the year anyway. It wasn't even frozen halfway across yet. But even when it's the middle of

January..." Vale House's receptionist was in her ideal element when she served as the hub of the local gossip network.

Leaning forward across her desk, Cally caught Bethany's eye through the open doorway and nodded to communicate that she'd successfully handled all her calls. Bethany, still chatting, returned a thumbs-up. At last Cally reached for her computer mouse to click and read the message waiting in the chat program.

Emerald << So have you decided what your wish will be?

"Ugh." She rested her hands lightly on the keyboard and tried to recall how to spell *"Et tu, Emerald?"*

"Oh! Cally!" Bethany's voice intruded again through the doorway. Cally looked back to see the receptionist with her hand over the mouthpiece of the phone. "You have a visitor!"

She glanced through her office window at the front lawn. The light was beginning to fade from the sky above the meadow, but it was still a little too early for Ben to be out there waiting for her. Maybe, she thought, her daughter and son-in-law had arrived in town early. She stood and went out into the Hall.

The young woman smiling quietly just inside the door was not Kelleigh, though she did call out "Mom!" when Cally entered the room. Rosheen had always called Cally "Mom," from the moment Brandon had introduced them, even though it had taken Cally a while to warm up to her potential daughter-in-law.

Rosheen swept across the Hall as if her feet barely touched the floor. Taking both of Cally's hands in hers, she said, "I just wanted to let you know. So you won't worry. He's arrived."

Cally glanced at Rosheen's middle. Adam had clearly not arrived yet, which was a good thing, since he was not due to be born until June. Rosheen laughed and pushed back her long, ash-colored hair. "No, silly. I mean Wes. Brandon's dad. He arrived at our house early this morning. I didn't want you to be afraid he might be the body they found in the pond."

Cally stood there grinning stupidly because she didn't want to admit this had not even occurred to her. And then she kept her teeth clenched a little longer, suddenly ashamed to hear her own disappointed voice flash through the back of her mind, ever so briefly, saying "Wouldn't that have been nice?" She was certainly no longer in love with Wes Edwards, but she didn't wish him ill. At least, she hadn't thought she did.

Finally she unclamped her jaw enough to say, "Oh. That's nice. I'm glad he found his way here okay."

"You should come over for dinner. Brandon's making vegan paella."

"Um, thank you, Rosheen, but no, I don't think that would be a good idea. Wes and I didn't part on the best of terms. I'm sure Brandon has told you."

Smiling gently, Rosheen shook her head. "Come on, Mom. I thought you two were grownups. There's no reason we can't all still be a family, even if you and Wes aren't married anymore. In fact it was Wes's idea to invite you!"

Bethany hung up the phone and came to Cally's rescue. "I'm afraid I'm going to need her here tonight," she called from behind the desk. "We were right in the middle of all this decorating, and it needs to get done in time for the party."

Rosheen cast an appraising look around the richly over-decorated Hall. She didn't look like she bought this excuse at all, but she nodded anyway. "I understand. Maybe we can all get together once Kelleigh and Gordon arrive."

"I think I might feel a bit more comfortable with that," Cally admitted.

This late in the year, the light outside was already fading quickly to dusk. Cally took her jacket from the coat rack next to the door and walked Rosheen across the lawn to the pillared gateway between the Vale House grounds and Main Street. Rosheen, she noticed, not only wasn't wearing a jacket, but had on footwear completely inadequate for the weather – more akin to ballet slippers than actual shoes. When they reached the curb, the young woman kissed Cally's cheek and crossed Main Street, passing like a dancer through the chilly shadows along Gardens Road to the third house down. There, she turned to wave before entering the warmly-lit Yellow House.

Cally stood awhile gazing at the lights in the windows, shivering in spite of her jacket. The Yellow House was a place she normally associated with love and peace. She shook herself and made a determined effort to hope Wes was finding the same there, tonight. She didn't need to harbor any grudges against him anymore. That would only have the effect of holding her back, and she was moving on with her life.

Yes, she thought, stepping back into the Vale House front yard to see a familiar silhouette leaning against the meadow fence, a familiar face smiling at her. She suddenly felt much warmer, and all thoughts of anything negative lurking behind her melted away as she smiled back at Ben Dawes. Yes, she was definitely moving on with her life.

3 – Early Nightfall

The sun set much earlier, these days, than it had back when Cally had first arrived in Woodley. That had been several months ago, but so much had happened since then, so much had changed in so many ways for her, she often felt like she'd lived here for many years.

One thing that had changed, certainly, was that Ben had entered her life. Though Cally had once sworn she would never love a man again, much less trust one, she had quickly fallen for Ben's steady and quiet presence and was happier now than she could remember ever being in her life.

One thing that had not changed since summer, though, was that Ben was still compelled to spend his nights, every night of his life, in his mother's kingdom: the faerie realm on the other side of the fence, beyond the horizon at the eastern edge of the meadow. Normally Ben's sister, Bree Dawes, who ran the family store in the downtown part of Woodley, would not have let him leave work this early. Bree's argument that he had to help her with the family business was the only technicality allowing him to visit the human realm at all, anymore. But even Bree had no say over when the sun rose and set, and Ben had to be in Faerie before the stars blazed full in the sky. As the days grew shorter and shorter, the time Cally could spend with him at the fence before he left grew shorter as well.

In addition to his silhouette, leaning on one elbow against the top rail in the way that had become so familiar to her, she also saw three horses grazing quietly on the other side of the fence near him. Two of them were a dark color; one shone pale silver in the moonlight. In sunlight, Cally knew, one of the darker ones would actually be more of a chestnut color.

"What are you scowling about?" Ben asked as she closed the

last few steps between them. Even with his back to the darkening sky over the meadow, the unusual china blue of his eyes shone like starlight; his warm smile showed through his silver-streaked beard.

She had to smile, then, too, nodding toward the horses. "I was just hoping we'd have some privacy, is all." She shook her head and leaned into his solid warmth, reaching up to trace the outline of his face with her fingertips. The horses paid them no mind.

His arms went around her and he drew her to him. He kissed her the way he always did, as if her lips contained the life-draught that kept him alive. When he finally drew back to look at her, he said, "I've missed you. I haven't seen you for...hours!"

She laughed, poignantly aware of all her reasons to be grateful. Maybe she couldn't see him on her own terms, or spend as much time with him as she would have liked, but she did get to see him, and that was more than many people had. To sweeten the deal, there were now the morning hours she would be able to spend with him, when he would return from beyond the meadow to creep into Vale House and up to her room, when they actually *would* have some privacy...

"Cally." His voice drew her thoughts back to the present. "Have you decided yet what your Christmas wish will be?"

"Oh, no." She stepped back and let her arms drop to her sides. "Not you, too?"

He threw a laugh up toward the moon sailing between ragged clouds above them. Leaning back against the fence, he reached out and pulled her close once more. "I've decided on mine." He kissed her eyes, one after the other, then the tip of her nose, and then her lips, once, briefly and sweetly.

"And what is *your* wish, Bennet Dawes?" She smiled playfully, hoping he would understand she wasn't really talking about Christmas wishes.

He shook his head. "That would be telling. We aren't supposed to tell, you know. Not even the people we love and trust most. That would cause the wish to not come true." His voice had grown serious, but even in the dim light Cally could see the fine crinkles that radiated outward from his eyes whenever he smiled.

"We'd better get going, Your Majesty," said a snarky voice

on the other side of the fence. Cally noticed, from the corner of her eye, that one of the darker horses had raised its head.

"Do you mind, Errin?" Cally didn't look away from Ben's face. "We're trying to have a moment, here."

"The queen doesn't like it when he's late," said the horse, stepping nearer. "Especially on nights when there's a celebration going on."

"There's always a celebration going on in Rianwynn's court. Except when there's a war going on, of course." Cally turned, finally, to look at the speaker. By the time the horse reached the fence, Errin had assumed the shape of a teenage girl with a wild mane of hair that shone bright ginger even in the moonlight.

"You're welcome to join us if you like." The mischief in the girl's green eyes belied her smile.

"I think I'll pass." The last time Cally had attended a celebration in Faerie, she'd felt like Cinderella at the ball, only still clad in rags and ashes.

"We'd be happy to give you a lift!" called the white horse, still in horse-form, from further out in the meadow.

"Thanks just the same." Cally knew Mima was deliberately taunting her. She looked back up at Ben instead.

He was grinning good-naturedly at the horses, but he tightened his arms around Cally as he answered them. "I'll be along in a moment," he said pointedly.

"Suit yourself!" Errin, stepping backwards, bowed deeply enough to him that Cally could almost swear it actually was a gesture of respect rather than mockery. In the midst of her bow, the girl resumed her equine form and rejoined her cohorts. The three horses turned together and headed off toward the dark eastern horizon, walking swiftly at first but shifting to a gallop until only their hoofbeats could be heard fading into the distance.

Ben's ever-patient smile, as he watched them, made Cally smile too. She really had wanted to answer the question he'd asked her, before they'd been interrupted, but she couldn't think of the right words to explain why the idea of wishing vexed her so much. She actually knew what her wish would be, if she could have it. If she really could have one wish, if wishes really could come true, she would wish for him to be able to spend his nights here with her, on the human side of the fence.

But that was not possible, no matter how much either of them might wish it. They were both too old, anyway, to live out the usual fairytale of young lovers marrying and raising a family. They both already had children and, in a weird twist of fate, they were even both expecting a grandchild – the same grandchild, as Rosheen was his youngest daughter – in a few months.

But, they weren't too old for the "growing old together" part of the story, if only... if only... She tucked her head under his chin and squeezed her eyes shut to stop the vision entering her head again. It always wrenched her heart: the sappy, unbidden vision of the two of them walking on along this very fence, down past the pond and across the field to one of the little cottages on Bells Road just like a normal couple might do. Rather than herself standing alone beside the fence every night, watching him disappear into the dark meadow.

That was the thing, she thought, sighing. They could never be a normal couple. Ben was only half human, and when he spent time in his mother's country, he didn't age. Someday, when Bree died, he would have to return there forever, and then he would never age or die. For her to wish for him to be released from his contract with Faerie, so that he could stay here with her, would be to wish for him to age and die like an ordinary human, and she could never wish that.

She pulled back enough to look up into his face again, arranging her own expression into the semblance of a philosophical smile. "Wishing only breaks your heart," she answered at last. "I have had more love and passion in the last few months than most women will ever have in their entire lives." She meant it. "I don't need to make any wishes."

He nodded, regarding her with his blue gaze, as if he understood. She felt him take several slow and deliberate breaths before speaking again.

"I understand you have a visitor."

"What?" The sudden change of subject confused her for a moment. "Oh! No, I'm afraid Kelleigh won't be able to get off work until the twenty-third."

"I look forward to meeting her. But..." He tilted his head, nodding past her toward Gardens Road. "I was referring to the father of your children. Kelleigh and Brandon's father."

"Ah. Yes." Him. She let out a breath so deep it was almost a snort. "Yes, he did arrive today, unfortunately."

Ben placed a hand on each of her arms and peered into her face as if to make sure she was looking at him. "Just so you know," he said levelly. "I'm not going to get all jealous and possessive, or anything like that. I understand you need to spend time with your family."

"I do," she had to agree. "And I will. I just wish he wasn't part of it."

He pulled her close to him again and wrapped his arms tight around her. She couldn't see his face, but she could feel the words rumbling up from deep in his chest as he said, "My love. Don't be too quick to dismiss family matters. Maybe it's not all it's cracked up to be. But I wouldn't know. I never really got to have a normal family."

She wanted to apologize for her cynicism, but his arms were so firm around her she couldn't really speak. He held her that way until they both realized he really was going to be late, once again incurring the wrath of the most powerful being in the Western hemisphere, once again due to his involvement with a mortal woman.

As the darkness of the horizon grew indistinguishable from the darkness of the sky, he stepped back and cupped her face in his hands. With one final, soft kiss he said, "I'll see you in the morning." Then he vaulted over the fence far more gracefully than a man his age should have been able to do.

4 – Dinner is Served

It always made Cally feel a little sad whenever she walked up the porch steps in the evening and didn't see the Captain's ghost sitting in his favorite wicker chair beside the door. But ever since Doug Arkwright's spirit had moved on, the old gray tomcat ghost, Doctor Boojums, seemed to have taken over his haunting duties. Boo lay curled up in the chair just as any living cat might, purring soundlessly and watching the moon pass overhead through great, silvery eyes.

She paused when she reached the top step. "I guess the cold doesn't bother you," she said (quietly, in case anyone might be listening.) The ghost cat squeezed his eyes shut briefly in reply. Then Cally heard a meow, which she knew could not have come from Doctor Boojums. He never made any sound. She turned to see another cat, a scrawny calico, standing near the front door.

"Oh! Cyndi, how did you get here? Our Nell must be visiting!" Cally hurried across the porch to open the door, since Cyndi Lauper was not a ghost and therefore could not pass through closed doors if humans were watching. The little cat ran between Cally's ankles into the house.

As Cyndi dashed around the desk and into the dining room, Cally locked the front door behind her. Bethany had gone home for the evening, but apparently Katarina and Ignacio had not, yet. The aroma of cooking food (something distinctly spicy, she thought) wafted through the Hall, and she saw Ignacio crouching in front of the fireplace, poking at a newly kindled fire.

"That looks cheerful!" She stepped closer to watch as he blew gently on the kindling, encouraging flames to dance higher between the logs. She admired his expertise, but she admired Ignacio's skill at everything. There wasn't anything he couldn't do,

17

and do well, if he set his hand to it.

It occurred to her that if anyone could actually be "the real Santa," it might be Ignacio. She squinted and considered his lean frame and long, black hair. He certainly didn't resemble anyone's traditional image of Santa Claus, but if he should ever tell her he could make reindeer fly, she would believe it.

"But how is Santa going to get down the chimney if we have a fire going?" The fireplace in the Hall shared its chimney with the much fancier fireplace in the parlor. Smirking mischievously she suggested, "Oh, I know! Maybe Santa can come down the chimney in Ian's quarters?"

"Don't you worry about how Santa will get into the house." Ignacio straightened and leaned the poker against the fender. "He'll manage just fine. Come on. Kat is making *arroz moro* for supper. You won't have to forage breakfast leftovers for your supper tonight."

She shook her head. "Ignacio, you and Kat don't need to feed me! I'm perfectly capable of scraping together a meal for myself."

"I'm sure you are. But Nell is visiting." Closing the fire-screen, he gestured into the dining room, where Nell's cat had disappeared. "Also, we're expecting company."

Cally looked through the wide doorway. Though the long dining table was covered with a white linen cloth as always, and with fir and holly centerpieces down the middle, she didn't see any place settings.

"Company?"

"*Si.* Doctor Tanahey called. He says he needs our advice about something. Well, Katarina's advice, anyway, and yours." He walked into the dining room and turned toward the narrow hallway off the north end of the room. "Doc is practically family," he said over his shoulder. "We just thought it would be cozier in the kitchen."

Cally couldn't help but smile as she followed him (the back hall was too narrow for two people to walk abreast) and asked, "Is this advice Doc is seeking, by any chance, about Bethany?"

"He didn't say."

"I bet it's about Bethany."

18

Around another corner to the left, the passage ended where a pair of swinging doors opened into a brightly lit, well-appointed kitchen, much more modern than the rest of the house. A young woman with unruly auburn hair was sitting at the work table in the center of the room, slicing radishes into a salad bowl. Katarina stood with her back to them at the industrial-size stove. The little calico cat had positioned herself on the mat directly behind the cook's heels.

"She better hope I don't trip over her and drop this whole pot on her head!" Katarina was saying.

"You don't fool me, Kat." Nell looked up and brushed her curls out of her eyes. "I know you love cats. And when I leave for school in January, you get to have Cyndi back here full time!"

Cally could see Katarina's shoulders tighten as she bit back whatever it was she wanted to say about that. Katarina and Ignacio had practically raised Nell, and Katarina, especially, had never liked the idea of Nell moving to her own apartment just down Main Street. She believed Nell's mental illness made her too vulnerable to be on her own, and now Ian May's daughter had got it into her head to leave Woodley altogether to attend college.

Before Katarina could embark on yet another campaign to try to talk the young woman out of this, Cally walked around the table to give Nell a side-hug. "To what do we owe this honor?"

Nell turned her wide, brown-eyed smile to Cally. "Tonight is Solstice," she said, as if that were a perfectly conventional reason for visiting the family home. "For faeries, that's like New Year's Eve."

Katarina put down her wooden spoon and crossed herself. "Well then I wish them a happy new year." She scowled into the pot for a moment before taking up the spoon again. "Just as long as they have it *over there!*" With a firm nod toward the east wall of the kitchen, she resumed stirring.

"I'm sure they will," said Cally. She wasn't kidding, but she didn't elaborate. Taking five dinner plates from a tall, glass-fronted cabinet, she began distributing them around the work table. "So where's all this snow we're supposed to be getting?"

She could see, through the window above the sink, that

19

Ignacio had switched on the light outside the back door. She expected Doc would be arriving that way, but she didn't see a single flake falling in the illuminated back yard. "Santa can't very well land his sleigh on the roof if there's no snow on it, now, can he?"

Cally was new to the South. This would be her first Christmas in North Carolina and she had grown up under the impression Christmases here were green and warm and sunny. October and November had disabused her, by now, of the notion of wearing shorts and sleeveless tops during the winter months, but she still couldn't convince herself to expect the white Christmas everyone at Vale House was promising.

Ignacio answered her question about Santa as if it had been serious. "It rarely snows this early in the season," he explained patiently. He was snipping sprigs of cilantro from the box-garden Katarina kept on the windowsill; the fresh aroma rising from it made the kitchen smell more like summer than winter. "Usually we get our first snow later in January, or early February. If at all. Some years we never get any at all. Except thanks to Sofie, even if it's not snowing anywhere else in the country on Christmas Eve, it always snows here in Woodley."

"Thanks to Sofie?"

"Oh, yes," Nell put down her paring knife. "Snow for next Christmas is always Mama's Christmas wish to Santa. When the snow falls this year, it will be from her wish last year." She held up one hand, palm upward, as if to demonstrate. "Then she'll make the same wish again, only for next year." She held up her other hand, nodding as if that explained everything.

Cally paused with the last plate in her hands. "That would mean Sofie always got to speak with Santa, even before. When she was...you know...confined to her quarters. So that means Ian must be the one playing Santa!"

This was met with laughter all around, particularly from Nell. "Don't be silly, Cally," she said. "Dad can't grant wishes!"

Cally saw the logical flaw in her deduction, but she stopped herself from saying, "Well, nobody can, after all." She quietly set down the final plate.

The door flew open and a silver-haired man burst through.

He shut it quickly behind him as if wolves were chasing him. Greetings of "Hello, Doc!" and "Evening, Daniel!" arose from everyone in the room.

Cally briefly considered whether it might be Doc who would play Santa for the Christmas party. His hair was close enough to white, after all, and he had the right build for it. He even wore a jolly smile as he blustered, "I can't believe how cold it is out there!" He rubbed his hands together to warm them a little before accepting Ignacio's handshake. "Won't be surprised if we get snow tonight."

"Probably not tonight," Nell reasoned, returning to chopping salad ingredients. "After all, Mama and Daddy aren't back yet."

"I'll tell you what." Doc paused in the middle of taking off his jacket, his face suddenly somber. "When I first heard about that body in the pond, I was afraid it might be Ian..."

"We all were!" Katarina interrupted. She turned around from the stove with a heavy, covered caldera between her mitted hands. "But let's not talk about things like that while we're trying to eat!" She successfully negotiated the cat underfoot and placed the pot in the middle of the work table. "Have a seat, Daniel. Your timing is perfect!"

Doc climbed onto the stool next to Nell's. "That smells heavenly," he said, inhaling deeply as Ignacio removed the cover from the pot. Cally craned her head to look into the caldera of rice and black beans which almost looked red thanks to all the cayenne powder Katarina had added. Katarina only skimped on spice when serving out-of-town guests.

"So, not tacos," Cally observed with a grin.

"Hmph." If Katarina hadn't known Cally was teasing her, she might have said something worse. "I only make tacos once a year, for the Christmas Eve party. You'll soon find out what a *real* taco is, and then you won't joke anymore!"

Still grinning, Cally sat down on the opposite side of the table while Ignacio opened one of the refrigerators to retrieve a pitcher full of a creamy, orange-tinted beverage. "This," he said, setting it on the table next to a stack of tall glasses, "is just in case."

"Just in case what?" Doc began filling his plate.

"You'll find out." Cally put a small serving of *arroz moro* on her plate and poked it warily with her fork. She managed to get the first mouthful chewed and swallowed before she had to reach for a glass. Extinguishing the fire in her mouth with a sip of Ignacio's magical mango drink, she said, "It's good, Kat." Her voice came out husky and breathless. "It really is. Thank you."

"I concur!" Doc devoured several mouthfuls of the nuclear beans without so much as a wince. "Katarina Munoz, you are a master chef!"

Katarina laughed. "I'm glad you like it! Now what was it you wanted our advice about?"

Wiping his mouth, Doc folded his napkin carefully and laid it beside his plate. "Well, what I wanted to ask you, what I wanted to talk to you all about..." He paused with a finger in the air, looking past them to the closed doors leading to the back hall.

"It's alright," Katarina assured him. "Bethany has gone home for the evening."

"And we promise we won't tell," Cally added, testing another nibble of Chernobyl-in-a-pot. The dish really was tasty, she had to admit. Even through the heat, she could detect the subtle flavors of the herbs from the windowsill garden. She wondered if she should just keep eating without drinking, so that she might toughen up and get used to the spice, the way Katarina and Ignacio – and, apparently, Doc – were.

"Okay." Doc stood up to rummage in his pockets. "Well." Withdrawing a small object, he set it on top of his napkin. "It's this."

"Oh, cute!" Nell picked up the little wooden box, holding it at an angle so everyone could see the intricate carvings and inlaid gems on the lid.

Cally agreed it was on the very pretty side of cute. "Did you get it from the Wyrd Systers shop?"

"I did, and they said..."

"It's empty," Nell observed. She showed them the interior, lined with dark green velvet.

"Well, that's the thing." Doc sat back down and picked up his fork, but he did not resume eating. "I need your advice about what to put in it."

"For Bethany," Cally assumed.

"For Bethany." Doc's face flushed, and Cally knew it wasn't due to the spicy food.

"Hmm, well." Katarina tapped the tabletop with her fingers. "It would have to be something small! Like jewelry!"

"Yes, but..." Cally understood why Doc seemed to find the topic awkward. "It can't be too personal, or too expensive. Bethany still isn't sure how she feels about Doc courting her."

Doc's face was now completely red, but he soldiered on anyway. "Right. Exactly. I don't want to come off as pushy, or scare her off. She's a lady, after all! But, well...I also need to let her know how serious I am. Neither of us is getting any younger, and we may not have that much... I mean, I just wish..." His voice trailed off into silence. Cally's heart went out to him. She understood, herself, how short life could seem when you wished you could find a way to spend it with someone you loved.

"Well, there's your answer." When nobody spoke for several moments, Nell finished Doc's thought for him. "You need to wish. Have you made your Christmas wish yet?"

"Oh, but..." Doc fidgeted with his flatware and regarded the ceiling. "No, I couldn't. We aren't allowed to wish for something that would interfere with someone's free will. And even if we could, well, I wouldn't do that to Bethany. I want her to... you know... choose me herself."

"She's *loco* if she doesn't!" Katarina twirled a finger around her ear to illustrate.

Everyone had to laugh at that, but it didn't solve Doc's dilemma.

Nell brushed her hair out of her eyes and laid a gentle hand on Doc's arm. "You just think awhile, Daniel Tanahey. You just think about it. The answer will come to you." Cally stared at the young woman in wonder, and not for the first time. Nell was by far the youngest person in the room, and her condition often made it difficult for her to navigate everyday life, but sometimes she seemed to be the oldest and wisest among them. "You'll figure out just what to wish for. It will be the right thing, and it won't have to impinge on anyone's free will at all."

Cally nodded at the wisdom – or at least the kindness – of

Nell's words, so in agreement with them that she barely noticed how, as Nell spoke, she turned her eyes from Doc and seemed to be speaking directly to Cally instead.

5 - The Ghost of Christmas Presents

Doc, after helping to clean up the kitchen, walked Nell and Cyndi Lauper back to their studio apartment above the coffee shop, and Ignacio and Katarina went home to their little cottage in the back of the garden. Cally made her way to her office, switching off lights as she passed. By the time she reached the Hall, the Vale House downstairs was illuminated only by the lighted china cabinet in the dining room and the green-shaded lamp on the reception desk – and the gaudy string of colored lights Bethany had wound into the potted ficus beside the front door. She paused a moment with her hand on the office doorknob, considering whether or not she should unplug them for the night.

"I love Christmas!"

She turned around to see the skinny young ghost still wearing his Santa hat. He was sitting behind the desk, trying (apparently) to make the office chair spin. He was not succeeding, but he wore a wide, happy smile across his face.

"So many colors!" he said. "So much light!"

"Alright, then, Georgie. I'll leave them on for you."

Like so many people Cally had met since she'd arrived at Vale House, she'd come to love this ghostly member of her found family. Many times she had wished there were some way she could hug him, but George's powers of manifestation were limited to the visual and aural (for those who could see and hear ghosts, anyway), a bit of interference with electronic devices, and a dubious fashion sense.

"What are you going to wish for when Santa Claus comes?" he asked her, then looked down at his improvised Christmas outfit. "The real Santa, I mean."

Cally knew George had been haunting Vale House for nearly

25

half his life which, including the years he'd been dead, totaled about four centuries. "So you're saying Santa really is real? You've seen him?"

"He *is* real!" George stopped trying to spin the chair and nodded solemnly. "He comes to the party every Christmas Eve. But I've only ever glimpsed him. He mostly stays in the parlor, and I can't go in there. It's too far away from my *zemi*."

"And what would you wish for, if you could go into the parlor and talk to him?" Cally had been trying since October to think of a way to demonstrate to George that he wasn't as bound to his *zemi*, the little wooden carving he'd owned in life, as much as he believed he was. It occurred to her that revealing this as the answer to his Christmas wish might be fun for both of them. "What if I carry your *zemi* into the parlor for you? When Santa is there. What might you ask him for, then?"

She thought it was painfully obvious that he should wish, if he could, to be freed from the constraints of his *zemi*, but George had other things on his spectral mind. "I would wish for a computer of my own!" he declared with a resolute nod.

Cally had to laugh. "George. What do you need a computer for?"

"Well you told me never to mess with yours, and I promised not to. Anyway I don't like that room you keep it in." He tilted his head toward her office door. "But if I had my own computer, the whole world would be open to me! I could go anywhere I want without ever having to be more than a step away from my *zemi!*"

She was moved by the yearning in his voice. It had to be awfully tedious, she thought, to be stuck haunting the same corridor, stairway, and Reception Hall year after year. She was tempted to just tell him the truth right then, to run upstairs and get his *zemi* out of the drawer of the butler's desk and throw it outside to show him it had no real power over him. But she knew if she did that he would only follow it into the lawn, so convinced was he that he could never get more than a few yards away from it. She needed to think of a way to show him in no uncertain terms that he could exist perfectly well without it. The Christmas party, whether or not the attending Santa was real, might be the ideal opportunity. The wheels in her mind began to churn so that she barely noticed when George doffed his Santa hat and vanished.

When she finally slipped in to her office, she saw the unanswered message still patiently blinking in the corner of her computer screen. "Sorry, Em," she murmured under her breath. "I'll be with you in a minute." She bent to remove the office key from her desk drawer. This she carried out into the Hall, where she tucked it into the mulch around the bottom of the merrily twinkling potted ficus.

Returning to the office, she locked the door from the inside. Then she picked her laptop up from the desk and carried it to the closet at the side of the room. A spiral stair rose from this closet to the bedroom – her bedroom – above.

The Dogwood Room, which Bethany had decorated in tasteful creams and greens, was spacious if a bit crowded with antique furniture. Its tall casement windows overlooked the front porch. The moon was no longer visible through these, as it had passed over the roof of Vale House and was now advancing behind it into the west. Cally opened one of the windows just enough to let in some fresh, chilly air. She was inclined to agree with George that the office below seemed somehow unpleasant and stuffy but, with the window open a crack, this part of the suite held more than a few pleasant memories.

She changed into a warm, flannel nightgown and threw the dogwood-blossom shaped pillows from the bed onto the green chair beside the dresser. Then, crawling under the covers, she laid her computer on her knees and opened it. When she clicked the message icon, however, a dialog box appeared informing her there was *No Internet Service Available.*

Sighing with annoyance, she climbed back out of the bed and opened the door into the upstairs hallway. She had become accustomed to spending her nights alone in a huge haunted house, but she still wanted to avoid ghosts – one of them, in any case – on this particular quest. Looking left and right along the corridor of closed guestroom doors, she made sure George wasn't watching. He'd often claimed to have a great talent for manipulating electronics, but she was about to perform a trick she did not want him to learn.

She dashed barefoot the length of the hallway, past the gallery overlooking the dining room, all the way to the narrow white door across the hall from the Azalea Room. Opening this little electrical closet she regarded all the green, yellow and red lights winking silently amid the cobwebs. Ignacio had demonstrated to her, when she'd become Vale House's office manager, how all the Wi-Fi equipment worked, explaining which sleek, plastic box was the modem and which the router, and what each of the lights meant, but she couldn't remember any of that. She did, however, remember the main thing he'd shown her.

Reaching behind the electronics into a tangled nest of wires and cords, she found the main power strip and switched it off. All the little lights went out. After counting slowly to ten, she flipped the switch back on again. The lights winked back to life one by one and, when she was satisfied that more of them were green than had been before, she shut the door.

Arriving back in the doorway of the Dogwood Room, she caught sight of her own reflection in the mirror above the dresser. Dressed all in white with pale hair flowing behind her, standing in the hallway with the gallery railing at her back, she wondered if she might be turning into Vale House's next nighttime-wandering *Lady in White.*

6 – A Chat with Emerald

The time-stamp on the message from Emerald showed it had been waiting, unanswered, for almost twelve hours. Emerald had been a faithful friend for many years, having supported Cally through some of the most difficult times of her life, and she deserved quicker replies than this.

Though there was no guaranteeing Emerald would still be logged on now to see it, Cally took a deep breath and began typing her reply into the old-fashioned text-chat program. By way of apology, she cobbled together a brief account of her hectic afternoon including the body in the pond, Wes's arrival, and the unexpected dinner in the kitchen. She concluded with her standard defense in reply to Emerald's original question:

> **Cally>>** Anyway, Em, I don't really believe in wishing.

She expected, then, to just try to get some sleep and await a reply in the morning, but Emerald's reply came almost immediately.

> **Emerald<<** But you believe in ghosts
>
> **Cally>>** That's like saying I believe in computers. Or cars. Of course I believe in things I can see!
>
> **Emerald<<** LOL you mean like me? But you have never seen me
>
> **Cally>>** I've seen gigabytes of messages from you, and I prefer to think I'm not imagining all of them.

29

> **Cally>>** But tell me, Emerald: What would YOU wish for, if wishes could come true?
>
> **Emerald<<** Well since you ask - - I would wish for exactly that - - to know whether I am real or not
>
> **Cally>>** Of course you're real. Don't be silly.
>
> **Emerald<<** But you have never seen me

It was true. Though Cally and Emerald had "met" in an internet discussion group many years ago, they had never yet met in real life, and Emerald had never so much as posted a photograph of herself. For a while, Cally had suspected Emerald might be a ghost, a spirit haunting the internet for whatever reason, like the ghost of Melissa who haunted the old console television downstairs. But that didn't add up. Most ghosts Cally had met (and she'd only recently begun to understand she'd actually met quite a few) could at least remember something about their past. Often it was the only thing of which their consciousnesses were cognizant. Yet Emerald's memories were, by her own account, sketchy at best.

> **Emerald<<** Sorry Cally - - I wasn't trying to get all existential on you
>
> **Emerald<<** I was just pointing out - - you do believe in things you can't see!
>
> **Cally>>** Of course. You are right. And yes, of course I believe in you.
>
> **Emerald<<** And I believe in you, my friend
>
> **Cally>>** Do you know what a Floppy Disk is?
>
> **Emerald<<** What?
>
> **Emerald<<** I mean yes I remember what floppy disks were - - but why are you asking?
>
> **Emerald<<** I don't see what they have to do with it! Or are you just trying to get me to reveal my age? :)

Cally>> Hah! No. But your existentialism reminded me of something. Do you remember that story you wrote and sent to me?

Emerald<< I do - - but to be honest with you I'm not even sure I wrote it - - and that's the truth

Cally>> Well that makes sense.

Cally started to type the reason why it made sense, but then she took her hands off the keyboard. She had been procrastinating for months over telling Emerald about the old floppy disk Bree Dawes had given to her. Luke (who, in addition to selling pizza, ran a computer repair service out of his shop) had recently helped her extract the data from it, and it had turned out to be another copy of almost the exact same unfinished story, word for disjointed word, that Emerald had sent to her as a text file over the summer. Bree remained unwilling to tell Cally how she had come across the floppy, and Cally had begun to suspect Bree had actually written the story herself. The only conclusion she could draw from this was that Emerald was the main character, trapped in some kind of weird computer limbo because her author had never finished writing the story.

This idea was ludicrous, of course, and she wasn't certain about any of it. She really shouldn't, she realized, say anything to Emerald until she had all the details...

Emerald<< Cally? Why does it make sense? What makes you think I couldn't have written that story?

Cally>> Because your grammar is much better than what's in that text file!

Emerald<< You have a point

Cally>> Your punctuation is still pretty bad, though. ☺

Emerald<< Hah - - is that what you wanted to

31

talk to me about oh dearest and bestest of friends?

Cally>> As long as I don't have to talk about wishes, or believing in Santa.

Emerald<< Listen - - when you live in a place that literally has faeries crawling out of the woodwork it's only politic to comply with local customs

Cally>> How about if I wish for everyone not to make me make wishes?

Emerald<< Nice try but that's one thing you can't wish for

Emerald<< You can't wish for more wishes and you can't make a wish that interferes with anyone's free will

Emerald<< Seriously - - what's the big deal? What's your problem with wishing?

Cally>> It's not that I don't believe wishes can come true. It's because sometimes they do. I've come to regret things I've wished for in the past.

Emerald<< You're talking about your ex - - aren't you?

Cally>> I guess you're right.

Cally>> Sorry. I thought I'd left all that baggage behind me long ago.

Emerald<< Maybe it's just weirding you out having him visiting so nearby

Cally>> Oh, it is!

Cally>> But really, it's a good thing. He's trying to be a part of his children's lives again.

Cally>> Brandon and Rosheen seem very happy about it. I know Kelleigh will be over the moon.

Emerald<< You have a bright future ahead of you Callaghan McCarthy - - and a frankly lovely present

Emerald<< You shouldn't let the past keep tainting it

Cally>> I knew you were going to say that.

Emerald<< And you know I'm right

Cally>> I don't know, Em. It's dangerous to make bargains with faeries. And isn't that just what wishing is? Especially around here.

Cally>> This past October, on All Hallows Eve, Sofie wished for Ian to be able to go sailing like he always wanted to do. And for all intents and purposes it looks like he got to do exactly that. But I keep waiting for the other shoe to drop. There's always a price to pay.

Emerald<< Not at Christmas

Emerald<< A Christmas gift is a gift - - no strings attached

Cally>> Sorry. I'm tired and rambling. I'm sure I'll have a more positive attitude in the morning.

Emerald<< I know you will - - and we both know why!

Emerald<< So you better get some sleep while you can 😊

7 – Late Dawn

The sun rose later in winter, and on this short day it rose much later than it would for the entire rest of the year. By the time Cally woke in the gray light of dawn, aromas of coffee and breakfast were already wafting through the house. She could already hear the sound of soft footfalls on the stairs in the back of her closet. Throwing back the covers, she hurried to remove her computer, mouse, and notebooks from the bed.

As she was stacking all of her slept-upon office paraphernalia on the dresser, she saw Ben's reflection in the mirror, closing the door to the spiral stair behind him. He laid her office key on the dresser next to her other things and wrapped his arms around her from behind.

"I just remembered," she said, crossing her arms over his and regarding their reflection. "I did make a wish once, and it did come true. And I have not come to regret it." She successfully stopped herself adding the word "yet" to her sentence.

"Oh?" He loosened his arms enough to let her turn around and look at him directly. "And what was that?"

"I wished I could wake up with you in my bed."

He laughed, not too loudly, even though there were no guests staying at Vale House for whom to be quiet this morning. "Well, then, you should have stayed in bed a little longer!"

This was easily rectified. Cally knew Katarina would keep breakfast warm for them. Mornings at Vale House were peaceful, idyllic, especially since they now involved Ben. She found herself, more than once, almost daring to wish these moments could last forever, though she knew that was the most dangerous kind of wish of all.

When they finally descended the main stairs to the Hall,

Bethany looked up from the desk and met Cally's eyes but pointedly did not smirk, just as she had pointedly not smirked every morning since October.

"Join us for breakfast?" Ben asked, just as he had every morning since October.

Normally Bethany declined this offer, as she was not a breakfast-eater, but this time she picked up her coffee mug and said, "I do think I need a refill."

While Bethany forwarded the house line to her cell phone, Cally scowled at the specter standing in front of the desk. This ghost, also, was male and thin, but it was altogether unlike George. Cally didn't know his name; she had come to refer to him as The Preacher because of his sober demeanor. He was probably the only ghost she'd met so far that she didn't like, even though he'd never done anything except occasionally stand there staring morosely at the framed portraits of Lionel and Isbel May above the fireplace. Neither Bethany nor Ben could see ghosts the way Cally did, but she could tell they felt uncomfortable in The Preacher's presence, too. Bethany hastily gathered her mug and cell phone and led the way to the kitchen.

Silvery daylight filled the window over the kitchen sink, and Katarina sang something in Spanish as she dashed between stove and work table sans Cyndi Lauper underfoot. Doctor Boojums sat on the counter beside the sink (something Katarina would never have allowed a living cat to do) gazing through the window to where they all could see Ignacio throwing bread crusts to the chickens in the yard.

"That smells delicious!" Ben held out a chair for Cally, and then sat down as well. "What is it?"

Katarina laughed. "As if you care!" She put on a thick pair of oven mitts. "I think you'd eat leftover scraps if I fed them to you!"

Breakfast at Vale House was the only opportunity Ben ever had to enjoy a real, home-cooked meal. Before October, he had always made do with granola bars, beef jerky, and cold sandwiches from the cooler at the back of the family store. Now Katarina always made sure to prepare a healthy breakfast for him, even on mornings when there were no Bed and Breakfast guests to serve.

"Eggs strata de Provence!" the cook declared proudly, producing a sizzling casserole dish from one of the big ovens. Both she and Cally watched contentedly as Ben served himself a heaping portion.

"Does smell good," Bethany conceded, refilling her mug from the pot on the counter but not taking a plate for herself. She sat down at the work table with Ben and Cally, laying her cell phone beside her cup. "Have you heard anything new from the sheriff?"

Katarina gave her a stern "we don't talk about dead bodies at the table" look. Bethany scowled at her phone. Apparently, Cally realized, Bethany's status as the heart of the Woodley gossip grapevine was at stake here.

Ignacio came through the door and set a basket of brown eggs beside the sink, narrowly missing Doctor Boojums. "Sheriff Mahon's on his way," he said, as if he'd heard Bethany's question. "Just saw him park his car out by the street."

Katarina got out another coffee mug. Through the window, Cally could see Dunn Mahon coming into the back yard through the little wooden gate at the rear of the grounds. He paused outside the door to wipe his feet, but he didn't need to knock, as Ignacio was already opening the door for him.

Taking off his hat, the sheriff accepted the full mug Katarina handed to him. "Thanks, Kat," he said, taking a deep sip, but he was looking over the brim of the cup at Cally.

"Chilly out there this morning?" she asked by way of greeting.

The sheriff nodded. "My daddy used to say, weather like this, it's actually too cold to snow."

"Oh, we'll get our Christmas snow," Bethany said. "Don't you worry about that!" Despite her cheery affirmation, the scowl on her face remained, except it had turned from her cell phone to the food still on Cally's plate. Ben had already finished his second helping. Cally quickly ate the last few bites of her strata, and she and Ben stood to carry their plates to the sink.

"Hungry, Dunn?" Katarina offered. "There's plenty."

Cally had to laugh (though she was careful to laugh silently) when she heard Bethany stifle a groan. More food being served meant more delays in getting the information for which her loyal network was waiting with bated breath.

When the sheriff answered, "No thanks," Bethany practically jumped out of her seat.

"So, Dunn! Did you check those keys, the ones from the pockets of the body in the pond?" she asked all in one breath. "Did you find out if they matched the abandoned car out on the interstate?"

"I did," he answered much more slowly. "And they did." He put his mug down in front of Doctor Boojums and turned to look again at Cally.

Bethany's face was a study in forbearance, though her voice was pitched a little high. "They matched! Great! So now you know the name of our John Doe...?"

Cally might have laughed out loud this time, if she hadn't started to wonder why Sheriff Mahon was still staring at her.

Doctor Boojums stood up, sniffing at the contents of the sheriff's cup as if considering trying to drink it. He sneezed silently and vanished.

"The car is registered to a Wesley Edwards," said the sheriff.

Bethany snatched up her phone to start relaying this information to her grapevine. Then she put it down again sharply and looked at Cally.

Everyone was looking at Cally.

"Isn't that...?"

Cally looked around at everyone looking at her. "Yes," she said. "That's the name of the man I was once married to. That's the name of Brandon and Kelleigh's father. I don't understand."

8 - Strata

T he body in the pond couldn't have been Wes Edwards," Cally explained to all the faces looking at her. "He's at the Yellow House right now. I mean...that's what Rosheen told me last night. You remember, Bethany. You were there." She looked from the sheriff to Bethany and back again.

"I'm on my way there to talk to him," the sheriff said. "I just thought I'd stop here and ask you a few questions first, Ms. McCarthy. When was the last time you spoke to your ex? Was he planning on bringing anyone along with him on his visit?"

"My children arranged their father's visit without my assistance," Cally said. She hated it when people referred to Wes as "her ex." She didn't want him to be her anything. "I haven't spoken with him since Brandon's graduation. We aren't *'still good friends'* or anything like that." She drew quote-marks in the air with both hands.

She thought she knew, though, what the sheriff was getting at. He was thinking the body in the pond must have been a friend of Wes's, and that Wes might be responsible for it being there. "Still, I don't think he would... I mean, he was disloyal, and tried to gaslight me whenever I caught him in a lie, but he wasn't dangerous or anything like that. I couldn't imagine him drowning someone in an icy pond and then continuing on his merry way to visit his family for the holidays."

At least, she didn't want to imagine that. She squinted, in her mind's eye, through the kitchen wall in the direction of Gardens Road. No. There absolutely could not be a murderer staying at the Yellow House with her children. She shook her head to clear it of such thoughts.

"Well, if you can think of anything I should know before I

41

talk to him, I'd appreciate it.

"Now, Ms. Chase." The sheriff turned his attention to the table and gave Bethany a stern look. "It would really help me a lot if you would please wait until after everything is settled before you speak to any of your friends about this."

Bethany's eyes grew wide. "I wouldn't dream of it, Dunn!" She held both hands in the air, away from her phone, to demonstrate how disinclined she was to touch it. "I wouldn't want to compromise your investigation in any way, or even... oh my!... possibly put you in danger!" The woman had gone from impatient to conspiratorial all in a moment. Cally had to hide her smile behind her hand. When Bethany finally did release the information she had now diplomatically agreed to hoard, Woodley's gossip network would accord her that much more esteem for having had the inside scoop on a clandestine investigation.

"Should I come with you to the Yellow House, Sheriff?" Cally offered.

"For now, I think it would be best if you don't. I'll be in touch if I need you for anything else." This last he addressed to everyone in the room before he put his hat back on and opened the door.

"Well, there's a nice Merry Christmas hello for you!" Katarina said as they all watched his retreating back through the window.

"I'm sure there's a perfectly reasonable explanation," Cally said. "I'm sure it's nothing." She had to struggle to keep her voice steady, because the egg strata now knotting in her stomach didn't feel at all like nothing. Katarina had been right about avoiding unpleasant topics of conversation at the table.

"Sheriff Mahon's a pro." Ignacio picked up the basket of eggs and carried it to the refrigerator. "He'll have it all straightened out before Christmas Day."

Cally hoped he was right. He usually was. She slipped a hand through the crook of Ben's arm. "I think I'll walk with you to work today," she said.

9 - The Family Business

The residential district of Woodley might have resembled a Currier & Ives painting, Cally thought, except for the lack of snow. She noted, as she and Ben walked along Main Street, that almost all of the stately older homes had been decorated with evergreen bunting fastened to porch railings with wide, red bows. It looked as if a neighborhood committee had come to a consensus on a set of parameters for tasteful, coordinating décor.

As they passed each home, its door would open to discharge a cat onto the porch railing. Cally knew this meant she was being watched, but it no longer bothered her as it had when she'd first arrived. Now it felt familiar, almost normal. The silent regard of all the denizens of this quirky little town gave her a sense of belonging she had never really experienced before.

"Where I grew up," she said, not bothering to keep her voice down, "everyone said it never gets cold in the South."

"We're not *that* far south." Ben gave her a sideways grin. "But I'll admit, it is a little unusual for the weather to be so chilly this early in the season."

Cally took a deep breath of the crisp air. "It still doesn't smell like snow, though." They reached the end of the residential district, passing from beneath the bare branches of oaks along the sidewalks, and continued onto the stretch of street that served as Woodley's downtown. "I wonder if Ian would say there's a name for that smell? Like the way he likes to tell everyone the word for the smell of rain."

"Some say snow smells like tin," was the best Ben could come up with.

"Except tin doesn't have a smell." She waved, out of habit, as they walked past the feed store, though the lawn chair on the loading dock was empty this morning. Merv Arkwright had stopped spending his days there when the weather had turned cool. Pausing to let a single car pass down the street, they crossed diagonally to where a wooden sign reading *'Dawes News'* hung above the door of a low, brick storefront.

"If we really do get snow in Woodley every Christmas," she went on, "do they also get it in Blackthorn? I mean, it's only a few miles down the interstate."

"Well, one version of Blackthorn is, anyway." Ben did not elaborate as he followed her up onto the curb in front of Dawes News.

"I wish we could go back to Blackthorn someday." Cally paused to turn and face him. "Or, I should say, to *Olde Blackthorne*. Those really were some good burgers."

He smiled, reaching past her for the door handle. "Maybe you should make that your Christmas wish."

Before he could begin yanking on the famously stubborn door, a young man with dark, curly hair appeared on the other side. He gave the bottom of the door a solid kick to un-stick it, then leaned out, holding it open for them.

"Morning, Ben," he said. "Hey, nice to see you, Mom!"

Cally stepped into the dusty warmth of the old shop and hugged her son. From the dimness behind the counter, an old woman's voice called, "Shut that damn door! I'm not paying to heat the whole neighborhood!"

"Good morning, Bree," Cally called back to her.

"Good afternoon!" Bree barked by way of letting Ben know he was almost two minutes late for work. The white-haired proprietor turned her attention to the newspaper she held up in front of her face. Ben shut the door.

Brandon took off his apron and handed it to Ben. "Ennilangr is out back with his truck," he said, "unloading cases of cold drinks. Probably no hurry to get them inside, though. It's not like they're going to warm up out there!"

Ben put the apron on anyway, kissed Cally's cheek, and headed for the delivery door at the back of the store. Brandon bent down to pick up a wicker shopping basket full of, as far as Cally could tell, about twenty pounds of junk food.

"Just grabbed a few things for Rosheen," he explained, heading for the counter. "If I hadn't seen the ultrasound myself, I'd swear she's eating for at least three. Her appetite just keeps growing."

Cally tried not to be jealous that Rosheen had still never suffered so much as one single second of morning sickness. She followed Brandon to the register. "How are things going with your dad's visit?" she asked as nonchalantly as possible.

"Great! Rosheen really likes him! I get the feeling he really is trying to make up for the past."

Cally glanced out the store window. "Yes, well, about that..."

"So you'll be heading straight home, then." The white-haired old woman put her paper down. Brandon unloaded the basket, piling bags of gummy candy and cheese popcorn beside the register.

"Yes, Ma'am." Brandon's cheerful nature never paled in the face of Bree's gruffness. "Don't worry, I didn't leave too much work for Ben to do."

"Place is still awfully dusty," Bree observed. "And that door still sticks." She jabbed with bony fingers at the keys of the antique register.

Cally looked along the wooden shelves ranked throughout the dim interior. The place was always dusty, even immediately after it had been dusted, and "that door" had been repaired many times but still always stuck. It was as if the entire shop existed somehow in an odd fold of time, stuck between the pages of a history book that had been slammed shut at least fifty years ago.

Merchandise did seem to move freely in and out, however. Brandon added two boxes of toaster pastries to the pile beside the register. "I promised Rosheen I'd be home on time, today," he explained. "So she won't have to entertain Dad all by herself."

"Yes, Brandon, well..." Cally touched his shoulder to draw his attention back to her. "You might find, when you get home, well, you might find that Sheriff Mahon is there."

Brandon said a word Cally had once endeavored to prevent him from learning. "What? What's wrong?" He turned to bolt for the door, leaving his groceries behind.

"No, Rosheen is alright!" Cally grabbed his arm as he flew past. "Everyone's alright! The sheriff just wants to ask your father a few questions, is all."

Brandon let out a sigh and turned back to Cally, but his face had fallen. "Oh. Oh, of course. I should have figured he wasn't just here for a friendly visit. Who's husband did he piss off this time?"

"It's nothing like that, I'm sure." Cally was not sure at all, but she went on anyway. "Just that they found his car outside of town, abandoned on the shoulder." She didn't mention where they had found his car keys.

"Oh! Well, that's good, then!" Brandon's smile returned as he started piling the items Bree had rung up back into the basket.

"Good?"

"Yah. Dad said someone carjacked him out there on I-85, while he was on his way here. He couldn't find the exit into Woodley, so he pulled over and stepped out of his car to try to get a cell signal." Cally nodded. She'd done the same thing the first time she'd tried to find Woodley. "A car that was driving by stopped, and someone got out. He thought they were stopping to offer him a hand, but instead this guy jumped in his car and drove away with it."

"Oh, that's awful!" Cally couldn't help but feel sympathetic, even if it was toward Wes Edwards.

"So then he spotted the Seven Forks Diner and went inside for directions. Raven and Willow told him how to find the Yellow House, and it's a good thing they give good directions, because by the time he made it to our door, he was almost frozen stiff."

"Well, that explains it," Cally said, though she wasn't completely sure it did. Something seemed off about the story, something she couldn't quite put her finger on. But that, she supposed, was probably because she had become so accustomed in the past to none of Wes's stories ever adding up properly. At least the sheriff wouldn't be clapping her children's father into handcuffs and dragging him off to jail right before Christmas. "Okay, well, I guess you'd better not keep Rosheen waiting." She reached up to hug Brandon, but she still felt distracted about Wes's story. "Do you... do you think Rosheen and your dad would mind if I join you for lunch?"

Brandon laughed. "Of course not! We missed you at dinner last night. Though maybe it was just as well – Rosheen ate what would have been your portion. Hey, maybe we should stop and grab a pizza from Luke's shop?"

"She'll join you in a few minutes," Bree snapped from the other side of the counter. "I need a word with her first. By the way, that'll be five bucks."

Brandon and Cally both looked at the overflowing basket. "Are you sure?" The little packet of *'All-Natural Vegan Jerky'* by itself cost five dollars and change.

"Employee discount," said the old woman, giving them both a bright, blue-eyed glare that defied argument. "Bring the basket back when you come in to work tomorrow."

10 – A Non-Talk with Bree

Cally had meant to accompany Brandon back to the Yellow House, but she decided it would be best to let him go on ahead while she found out what Bree wanted. Bree seldom had anything to say to her and, when she did, it was never nice. Still, listening might at least give Cally an opportunity to ask some pointed questions about the mysterious floppy disk containing Emerald's story.

She remained beside the register, waving to Brandon through the store window as he headed up the sidewalk toward Gardens Road. She could hear Ben and the delivery driver behind her, talking and laughing amid sounds of banging doors and heavy cases being set on the floor.

"Got a new shipment of books in," Bree muttered into the newspaper she had, once again, raised like a shield between her face and the world.

Cally turned to the revolving display of paperbacks which always stood next to the counter. There she was delighted to see, among the dusty old books everyone in town had already read and put back, a number of shiny new novels in the top rack. Above the foxed and dogeared copy of Cally's own first novel were two copies of her latest release. She picked one up and regarded it with a wry smile. Though she'd been given more input into the cover image on this one, she still wished her publisher had not insisted the heroine's blouse be so low-cut.

"Get anywhere yet with that little project?" Bree snapped from behind her paper. Cally guessed Bree was not talking about her next novel. She put the book back in the rack.

"If you're talking about the computer disk you gave me, then yes. In fact, thanks to the generous donation of some old equipment from Luke, I was able to read the contents. Turns out, it's kind of a story."

"Kind of a story. And?"

"Well, and I've seen it before."

That, to Cally's satisfaction, made Bree put down the newspaper and look at her. The old woman's eyes, the same unusual shade of blue as Ben's but framed by far more wrinkles, now bored into her instead. "Where could you have seen it before?"

Cally took a breath to give herself a moment to think. "A friend of mine sent me a little story a few months ago, over the internet." That seemed innocuous enough. "It's about the adventures of a young girl born in a magical land. It's a very rough draft, but almost exactly the same story as the one on the floppy disk."

"What's so rough about it?"

Cally thought Bree sounded offended – more than she usually did, anyway – as if she had written the story herself. She backpedaled quickly. "Oh, nothing, really. It's a fine story, it's just that...well, it isn't finished. It's only the first several chapters. Clearly whoever wrote it meant for there to be more."

Bree muttered something under her breath, looking past Cally's shoulder to the back of the shop. Cally followed her gaze to where the big, blond deliveryman was waving in their direction as he departed. Ben shut the door behind him and began unpacking cases, loading energy drinks and bottled tea into the coolers along the rear wall.

"Bree, here's the thing." Cally leaned across the counter to draw the old woman's gaze back to her. "I think you know more about that floppy than you're telling me. The label written on the disk said *'Emerald.'* I mean, I get it. That's the name of the main character in the story. But it's also the name of my friend, the one who sent me the story. And I'm sure I've never mentioned her to you before."

Bree's eyes kept flicking back to the rear of the store. Ben had stopped his work there and stood still, now, watching them.

When the old woman turned back again, her eyes had grown wide and moist. She didn't speak, but gazed earnestly into Cally's face, and Cally thought she could guess what she was trying to say.

Bree did not want to have this conversation where Ben might overhear.

Nodding, Cally returned to the rack of paperback books. "Thanks," she said in a loud aside. "It's kind of you to offer, but I already have several copies my publisher sent me."

Ben resumed stacking drinks in the cooler.

More quietly, she said to Bree, "I'll come back later tonight. After the sun sets."

They both knew she meant: after Ben had gone back to Faerie.

11 – The Yellow House

It was a little late for lunch, but Cally ducked around the corner onto Railroad Street anyway to pick up a pizza from Luke's shop. He recommended Rosheen's current favorite: an extra-large farmhouse cheddar with organic spinach and a blend of wild mushrooms. By the time Cally got back to the intersection of Gardens and Main with the warm, fragrant box in her hands, her stomach was growling.

When she turned right, toward the Yellow House, she could see Sheriff Mahon's patrol car still parked at the curb. The sheriff himself was just coming down the porch stairs. When he saw her, he tipped his hat and waited on the bottom step.

"You can report back to Bethany Chase that everything seems to be in order." Sheriff Mahon laughed lightly at his own joke, but the way he gazed past Cally into the distance made her suspect something on his mind might not be in order at all. "Ms. McCarthy, I wonder if I could impose on you for a favor?"

She balanced the pizza box on the stair newel with one hand and extended the other to him. "Sheriff, please call me Cally, and of course you can ask me a favor. I won't promise I can do it, but I'll try."

His eyes focused on her at last. "Call me Dunn, then." He accepted her handshake. "Cally. Yes, well. Wesley Edwards, on the whole, was cordial and cooperative. Presented his ID and car registration willingly." He tilted his head back toward the front door of the Yellow House. "I assume you've already heard the story about how he was carjacked?"

"Of course." She laughed. "This is Woodley. Everyone has heard it by now."

The sheriff didn't seem amused. "Well, there are some holes

51

in Mr. Edwards's story. I asked him if he would come with me down to the station, to see if the body we found in the pond might be the man who took his car. He was adamant that he would not do so – he almost became hostile about it. Do you recall him being overly squeamish about things like that?"

"I can't say that I do. But what do I know? I was only married to him."

He paid her wry grin no notice. "Well, the favor I'd like to ask of you is just that. Would you mind coming down to the station in Blackthorn today, to take a look at the body yourself? I'm hoping you might recognize it as someone you knew through him, once, perhaps an old friend of his. I realize this is a lot to ask. You are under absolutely no obligation to do it."

"Of course I'll do anything I can to help, Dunn. And I understand. Wes's stories always had holes in them, as far as I can remember. Mind you, I'm not sure I'd recognize any of his current friends or frenemies, but I'll give it a shot."

He nodded toward the pizza box. "You don't need to come right away. Enjoy your visit with the young folks. I'll be at my desk until four today." He lifted his hat again and headed for his car.

As Cally continued up the porch steps, she could see that Brandon and Rosheen had been decorating for Christmas, too, and had apparently found all their decorations in the attic of the old house. A 1950s plastic snowman stood smiling beside the door, and a tinsel wreath encrusted with small glass balls (and not a few cobwebs) graced the door itself. At the top of the steps, she nearly tripped over a heavy Christmas tree stand. It looked to be wrought of iron in the shape of the ugliest Santa and sleigh she had ever seen, with four rusted legs shaped like reindeer hooves. She managed not to drop the pizza as Santa's waving hand caught on the cuff of her jeans, tearing the hem as she passed by. She thanked him sarcastically and reached to knock on the door.

"Mom, you don't need to knock!" Rosheen was standing inside the door, already opening it for her. "Just come right in anytime! That smells delicious, by the way." She took the box from Cally's hands before she was quite inside. Like Vale House, the Yellow House had a central entry hall with a stairway rising from it, but the scale of both was much smaller and, Cally thought, cozier. The smell of the pizza mingled with other culinary aromas already filling the house – something Mediterranean, she guessed.

"Oh, I probably shouldn't have brought food. I didn't know you were already cooking!"

"Not a problem." Rosheen carried the pizza box into the small living room to the left of the entry. She placed it on an antique coffee table and sat down on the floor next to it. "Brandon's just starting some beans for supper. This should tide us over! Have you had lunch?"

Cally had not, so she joined Rosheen at the coffee table, though she sat on the couch instead of the floor. Rosheen was halfway through her first slice of pizza by the time Cally reached into the box for her own.

The only sign Rosheen was expecting a baby at all was her appetite. At the beginning of her second trimester she was still as thin as a scarecrow, delicate and frail in appearance though Cally knew, now, just how strong she actually was. As Ben's daughter, she was at least one quarter faerie, and probably more like three quarters, since her mother was originally from Faerie, though Cally knew little else about her. Being the child's incipient grandmother made Cally, by faerie law, officially part of the Daoine Sidhe royal family. Cally was still not sure how she felt about this, but then, she still wasn't sure how she felt about becoming a grandmother at all.

At least Rosheen seemed to genuinely love Brandon, she thought, warmed by the way the young woman's face lit up when he came into the room. "This is good!" she said, waving him over to join them.

"I'm still full from my first lunch, thanks." Brandon smiled at them both. "Hey, look what I found!" He set a dusty box marked *'Ornaments'* on the couch beside Cally. "All we need now is an actual tree. Dad and I are going to go look for one in a little while."

"I take it you're going to set your tree up in that ...antique... stand out on the porch?"

Rosheen, mouth full, shook her head emphatically. Brandon said, "Hah, no. *That* thing is staying outside! Maybe we can sell it on eMarket. Rosheen is allergic, you know."

Cally did know. Because so much faerie blood flowed in her veins, Rosheen could not handle iron or steel – which was the reason Brandon did most of the cooking.

Out in the entryway, the sound of footsteps could be heard descending the stairs. Cally's chest tightened. She knew that must be Brandon and Rosheen's houseguest. Making a conscious effort to breathe calmly, she mustered a little laugh. "You guys aren't making him sleep in the attic, are you?"

Both Cally and Rosheen – who could see and communicate with ghosts just as well as Cally could – knew the attic of the Yellow House was haunted with spirits that weren't always pleasant.

"No!" Rosheen laughed around a mouthful of pizza. "I wouldn't do that to him!"

"Pity," Cally murmured, standing up and looking through the doorway to see the figure of a man she had once had reasonable hopes of never seeing again.

"Callaghan." Wes Edwards strode toward her with both hands outstretched. "How nice to see you. You look beautiful, as always." He opened his arms as if to offer her a hug. She quickly stuck out her right hand and gave him a firm handshake instead.

"Wesley," she said. "You look well."

"Not bad for a human who's about to become a grandfather, eh?"

Brandon had got his height and curly, dark hair from his father. Wes's hair was, naturally, not as dark as it had once been, but there was something about his slightly hunched stance that made him look older than Cally had expected. She thought he seemed weatherworn, and not in an attractive way. It made her feel a little dizzy to realize that, while she did know his face, it had really always been that of a total stranger. Still, for a fleeting moment, she thought she saw something unsettlingly familiar in his eyes. Whatever it was felt like a pinprick in her heart, and it was gone before she could put a name to it.

"I hope I'm not intruding into your new life by showing up here," he said. Still hanging onto her hand, he smiled a smile that seemed just a little too wide. "I just thought, well, if I'm going to be a grandfather, I should try to make amends with my family. And what better time of year to make up for past mistakes?"

Cally pulled her hand out of his. "That's a nice thought," she said. It was too late to make up for his past mistakes with her, but she did sincerely hope his newfound sentimentality would give Brandon – and Kelleigh, when she arrived – an opportunity to normalize their relationship with their father. Satisfied that he was on the up-and-up after all, and not actually a murderer trying to cover up his crime, she started thinking up excuses to make her exit.

"I'm afraid I'm getting emotional in my old age," Wes was saying. "I already got little Adam a Christmas present, even though I know he won't be born until Midsummers Day."

Cally thought "Midsummers Day" was an odd expression for someone like Wes to use. Perhaps he had heard it from Rosheen. She followed his gesture to the end table next to the window, on which sat an engraved silver goblet with a red bow tied around its stem.

She didn't bother to point out that Adam would not be old enough for such a thing for many years. The child would be delighted with it regardless. She had met Adam once, before she was even aware he had been conceived. He was the kind of ...person... who was delighted with everything. "Very nice," was all she said.

"Imagine it hanging on the tree," Brandon said. "Mom, want to come with Dad and me to look for one?"

"You guys have fun. I need to head into Blackthorn. Um, to do a favor for someone." Cally turned and nodded to Rosheen, noting that now only half a pizza remained in the box.

Rosheen swallowed her food quickly. "Oh! Maybe you could let Dad ride with you, then? The sheriff says he can pick up his car at the impound lot after they get the prints off..."

"That won't be necessary!" Wes interrupted sharply, his smile twisting into a snarl. Cally took a quick step backwards. She wondered if this was a glimpse of the "hostile" demeanor Sheriff Mahon had mentioned. It wasn't one of the faults she remembered him having, but at least his adamant refusal saved her having to make up a reason not to give him a lift.

He grinned foolishly, then, gazing down at his hands. "Sorry," he said. "Sorry. I guess that carjacking business really upset me. I didn't think I was going to make it, for a while there."

"No worries," Brandon said. "You're fine. When we go look for the tree, we can swing by Blackthorn and get your car. Maybe they'll have trees at BigOrange Hardware."

Wes gestured through the front window toward the meadow. "I'd really rather go hunt for a fresh tree in the wild..." As he spoke, Cally edged toward the door, waving to Rosheen and Brandon and hoping to get outside before Rosheen could invite her to return for dinner.

It was Wes who interrupted her departure. "Let me walk you out. I need to talk to you."

Cally let out a sigh, probably not as inaudibly as she should have. The backs of her shoulders itched as he walked far too close behind her to the door. Once they reached the porch, she turned to face him, backing up several steps to put an arm's length between them. She was willing to give him a chance to say whatever it was he had to say, but she wanted to make sure her exit down the stairs was clear.

He reached out a hand, palm upward. Her instinct was to step back once more, but she held her ground and met his eyes.

"I seem to have a lot to make up for," he said. Then he lowered his hand and turned to look across the street into the meadow. "I am only human and can't change the past. But all this family stuff, the holidays and the baby, you understand. All this has made me see how much I threw away in my foolish lifetime. I just want you to know: I have never stopped loving you. I intend to win you back, if I can."

Cally held her tongue. She was thinking, "You wouldn't know love if it bit you on the ass," but she was an empathetic person at heart. She couldn't quite bring herself to kick a man while he was making himself vulnerable (or at least putting on a good show of it.)

Finally she said, "I'm really glad you want to be a bigger part of your children's lives now." She spoke as levelly and kindly as she could. "I know they want that, too. Brandon seems happy to see you, and Rosheen seems to be enjoying your company. I know Kelleigh will be ecstatic when she gets here tomorrow. As for me, I am happy with my life just the way it is."

He turned back to her and she saw it again – that flash of something unsettling but somehow familiar. She couldn't put her finger on it and, right then, she really did not want to.

"I understand," he said. "There is someone new in your life, now."

"That isn't the point!"

She didn't bother to remind him that she had lived quite happily for years without anyone, before she'd met Ben. She didn't want to discuss Ben with him in any case. Her personal life was no longer any of his business. She moved sideways to the stairs.

He stepped forward as if to block her way. Cally backed up until her heel bumped into the iron Christmas tree stand. She glanced down at it, making up her mind that if he tried to touch her she would brain him with it.

"I only meant..." He spread both hands in a pleading gesture. "Well, think how it looks to your children, you sleeping around in plain sight of their father."

Cally's jaw dropped. She could not believe those words had come from the mouth of a man who had cheated on and lied to her almost from the moment they'd met. She didn't want to stay in his presence long enough to argue with him about it.

"I'm about to become a grandmother," she reminded. "I'm old enough to sleep with whoever I want!" She pushed past him and headed down the stairs, rage flaring so red in her eyes she could barely see the steps in front of her.

"That's not what I meant!" he called behind her. "It's just, I'm hoping. That's all. I need to know I at least stand a chance!"

She hurried down the walkway to the street, turning left toward Vale House. As she passed the houses along Gardens Road, she could hear doors shutting.

"Great," she thought. "Now the whole damn town will be talking about this!"

12 – The Seven Forks Diner

B y the time Cally got back to Vale House, Ignacio had finished hanging green wreaths with red bows in all of the front windows. Now he stood on a ladder fastening fir bunting along the porch eave. "Snow will start tomorrow night," he informed her as she climbed the porch steps. She didn't argue, but smiled and nodded as she opened the front door. Ignacio was almost always right about the weather.

A small, tinsel Christmas tree now stood glittering in the center of the reception desk. Bethany herself was not at the desk; Cally peeked into the parlor to find her, and Katarina on a stepladder, stringing white lights on a fir tree at least ten feet tall and half as wide. Even without ornaments, it shone like a holiday-card vignette against the two wide windows where they met at the southeast corner of the room. The entire room smelled of fresh fir.

"We're just putting on the lights, for now, " Bethany explained. "All the party guests will decorate it on Christmas Eve."

"It's how we do it every year!" Climbing down from the ladder, Katarina opened a red cardboard box and began transferring ornaments from it to a bowl on the console table. "All our oldest and best friends arrive early, and we drink rum punch and hang ornaments!"

"I look forward to that." Cally was surprised and pleased to realize she actually meant it.

"And speaking of yearly traditions. See that?" Bethany turned around and pointed at the fireplace, which was much larger, on this side of the chimney, than the one in the Hall and framed with a beautifully carved white mantelpiece. A few family photos and the antique clock had been moved aside so that a red basket, shaped like a sleigh, could occupy the very center of the mantel. "That is where

58

you should put your wish, when you think of it. Which you really ought to do soon!"

Cally could see several rolls of paper, tied with different-colored ribbons, already stacked in the basket.

"I'm working on it," she said, then changed the subject. "I'll be heading into Blackthorn for a little while. Is there anything I can pick up for either of you while I'm there?"

"Yes, if you don't mind!" Katarina hauled an armload of tangled lights from yet another box. "Twelve pounds of flank steak!"

"Flank steak?"

"Yes, with plenty of fatty streaks throughout, if you can find it!"

"Twelve pounds?"

"There's going to be a lot of people eating tacos!" She nodded emphatically.

Bethany, searching through the lights for the end of the string, nodded also. "Ennilangr has already delivered the onions and fresh chilis and things like that. But you can't expect a man to pick out good flank steak."

Cally wasn't sure she was any judge of flank steak, herself, but she promised to try. She went back across the Hall to her office to collect her purse and the Vale House checkbook. There was no sign, on the computer screen, of a waiting message from Emerald, for which she was thankful. Accomplishing her errands and getting back in time to see Ben off this evening would be cutting it close as it was.

She waved when she drove past the News Store, though Ben's back was to her as he swept the floor. The end of town was all of two blocks further on. Here Main Street turned into a two-lane blacktop road which continued into a tunnel of trees and down a gentle slope. At the bottom, it crossed a narrow bridge and then rose again until she could glimpse the Seven Forks Diner through the bare branches ahead. Interstate 85 lay beyond the diner, on the other side of a belt of longleaf pine trees.

As she drew near the pines, she suddenly braked and turned sharply into the diner's parking lot.

The only other vehicle there was a dark gray motorcycle parked beside the door. Getting out of her car, she paused for a moment to regard the evergreen wall along the interstate. She could hear tractor trailers passing by beyond the pines, but she couldn't really see the road. She recalled that when she'd first come to Woodley, she hadn't been able to see the diner from the interstate, either. She'd passed the exit to Woodley at least four times in either direction before an odd circumstance had attracted her attention to it.

"Considering leaving town?" A man coming out of the diner had paused beside the motorcycle.

"Ha. Only for a little while." She wasn't sure why she had interpreted his conversational words as questioning whether or not she was fleeing Woodley for good. She had been fleeing when she'd arrived here, but she had gradually realized her days of flight were over.

He put on his helmet and flashed her a grin. "Be careful of that Christmas traffic," he said, fastening the strap under his chin. "You get used to light traffic, in these kinds of places. When you get back out into the world, it can be a shock."

She nodded distractedly as he started his bike and drove away. It was not until the sound of his engine had faded beyond the pines that she made up her mind to go inside the diner.

She had always found the inside of the Seven Forks to be calming and peaceful. Woodland murals decorated three of the walls, making the interior feel like a forest retreat. Now it looked like a winter forest retreat, because the proprietors had hung dozens – perhaps hundreds – of hand-cut paper snowflakes from the ceiling on strings of differing lengths. She couldn't help smiling up at them as she passed beneath.

"Just sit anywhere, dear!" called a woman's voice from behind the counter. Cally looked to see a short, roundly-built older woman with a head of gray curls dash out from the kitchen doorway. "Shall I bring you tea, or coffee?"

"It's okay... Raven?" Cally always mixed up the names of the two women who ran the place, but they never seemed to mind. "I can't stay. I just wanted to ask you a question."

"Oh! Yes! Well, then, let me get Raven to bring her cards!"

"No, no, um, Willow? It's alright, I don't need a reading or anything. It's not that kind of question." Cally could see another woman, taller and thinner with long, white hair hurrying toward her from the back of the diner. She was already reaching into her apron pocket for the tarot deck she always carried. *That* one was Raven, Cally tried to imprint on her memory once and for all. "I just wanted to ask if you've seen a man."

Both women laughed and put their arms around one another. "You just missed one!" said the shorter one. "He went thataway on his motorcycle. Why, are you getting tired of Mr. Dawes?"

Cally rolled her eyes. "Sorry. I meant a specific man. About this tall." She held her hand above her head. "About my age, with dark gray hair, and he would have been here very early yesterday or late the night before, on foot and asking for directions."

They looked at one another. "No, I can't recall that we did."

"We stayed open a little late to let Wing finish his chili-cheese fries," the taller one recalled.

"But he was our only customer that night."

"And we don't open 'til lunchtime on weekdays."

"Why do you ask?"

A sick feeling churned in Cally's stomach. "Well, that explains why I felt like there were holes in Wes's carjacking story," she said, not having meant to say it out loud.

"Always trust your gut," advised the shorter woman.

The taller woman stepped closer to her, unwrapping the tarot deck in her hands. "Have a seat, dear. You clearly have questions that need answering. Willow, would you brew up some pumpkin spice tea, please?"

Cally backed away. "I'd love that." She really would have. "But I don't have time. I need to get to Sheriff Mahon's office."

The tall woman – Raven – put the cards back into her apron. "Yes," she said, nodding thoughtfully. "Yes, I think that's a very good idea."

13 – Cold Meat

T he biker had been right about the traffic. The interstate was crowded with holiday travelers and eighteen wheelers, and Blackthorn (the modern iteration of it, anyway) was a tangled mass of four-lane surface streets with cars crawling, bumper-to-bumper, between big-box stores and fast-food strips. By the time Cally reached the far edge of the town, where a single, broad gray building served as both police station and county jail, her clenched jaw was starting to give her a headache.

She parked around the side of the building. Here, the Blackthorn police department had allotted a small office for the county sheriff to sit down and do his paperwork when he wasn't out on his rounds. Cally found Dunn Mahon hunched over a cluttered desk, frowning into a notepad. He looked up and smiled when she came through the door, however, and stood to offer his hand.

"Ms. McCarthy. I'm really glad you've come."

"You promised to call me Cally, Dunn." She clasped his hand anyway. "Listen, I've got some additional information for you. You know how we both thought Wes's story was a little off somehow?"

"Yes." He gestured toward a plastic chair wedged between the wall and two metal filing cabinets, but Cally didn't feel like sitting down. The sheriff went on. "It's just that whoever took Mr. Edwards's car apparently didn't go very far. I found it just outside town, not even half a mile down the interstate. When I heard his story, I asked Mr. Edwards about that. He said it must've been because he was almost out of gas. I don't know, something still didn't sit right with me, so when I got back here I went out to the impoundment lot to look at the car. Turns out, the tank is nearly half full. Now, I suppose the thief could have got some gas at the station just across from the Seven Forks, but Mr. Edwards would have seen that, if he was in the diner talking to Raven and Willow. Anyway it still doesn't answer the question of why the carjacker would have abandoned the car such a short distance away from the site of the theft."

"Well." Cally couldn't help feeling a little smug as she presented her own scrap of information. "I just talked to Raven and Willow. They say they've never seen Wes. Not that night, not ever."

The sheriff let out a puff of breath and ran his hand through his hair. Looking back down at his paperwork, he bent to make a note in one corner. "Guess I should go and talk to Raven and Willow myself, eh?"

Cally smiled, imagining them trying to talk him into a tarot reading. She looked around the tiny office. "So where's this famous cadaver?"

He led her back outside and around the corner to a steel door in the windowless back wall of the building. "The county examiner didn't find any signs of foul play," he told her as he unlocked the door. "He's sent the dental impressions in for a database search, and I sent in the prints from the car and the deceased, as well. Those sorts of things usually take a couple days to get back to us. Maybe a little longer because of the holidays."

Inside the door, he led her along a tiled corridor illuminated by flickering overhead lights. "Unless some relatives turn up to claim him pretty soon," he went on, "I'm going to have to transfer him to the facility in Raleigh for a full autopsy. Our John Doe not having died of natural causes and all. Have you ever done this before?" He had stopped in front of another steel door, this one with a small, wire-reinforced window at its top. His hand rested on the door handle, but he was peering into her face. "You sure you're going to be okay?"

"I've never identified a body," she had to admit. "But I've been to viewings at funeral parlors. I don't think it'll bother me."

"It isn't really the same." He opened the door for her anyway, and held it while she went through.

The little room that served as Blackthorn's temporary morgue was not like the ones Cally had seen on TV. It was more like a walk-in refrigerator, small and cramped and lined with steel shelves. The human-body-shaped mass lying on the chrome table taking up most of the room was not covered with a white sheet, but was inside a blue, zippered bag. The sheriff had to move a stack of boxes out of Cally's way so she could approach it (she did not care to speculate about what might be inside the boxes.)

"Alright, then." The sheriff pulled a pair of latex gloves from a box on a nearby shelf and put them on. "I really appreciate your doing this for me." He unzipped just enough of the bag to reveal the face inside. "Ring any bells?"

A very loud bell – large and made of cast iron, Cally thought – rang right through her bones, down to her feet and out through the floor. She did recognize the face. Though its skin looked as if it might be carved from gray soap, it was the same face she'd just seen in her son's house an hour ago. Right down to the hair that was now grayer and the face that was slightly heavier than she remembered from his youth, it exactly resembled Wes Edwards.

"Ms. McCar... Cally?" Sheriff Mahon drew the sides of the zipper together to conceal the face from her once more. "Are you alright? I'm sorry, I shouldn't have asked you to do this." He grasped her elbow and tugged her toward the door. "Let's get you to a chair."

"No, no, it's not that." She peered through the slit in the plastic, trying to make sure her imagination wasn't playing tricks on her. "It's just...Dunn, if I didn't know better, I would swear that is Wes Edwards."

He shook his head. "Well, we both know that can't be." Opening the bag again, he asked, "What about his close male relatives? They might look different, more like him, since you last saw them."

Cally did feel a little dizzy, wishing for the chair the sheriff had mentioned, but she bent over the waxy, gray face and looked closer. "Wes is an only child," she said. "Or was. He had a couple of uncles. They'd be much older than this by now, but..." She stood back and looked at the sheriff. "Can we try one more thing? If you could just unzip the bag a little further. About down to here." She placed the edge of her hand against her own left collarbone.

The sheriff did as she wished, and she leaned over to look at the cadaver's chest. Wes had had a tattoo, containing the name of an old girlfriend, done crudely at a party shortly before they'd met. He had refused to have it removed or altered, despite her protestations, even after they'd married, but she didn't see it there now.

"Okay, I guess you're right. That can't be him. But..." The swirls of hair on the body's chest did look like she remembered. "Or. Wait..." She bent closer. "There does seem to be a scar there. But it's so pale... No. It looks like him, but it can't be." The longer she looked at the waxy, gray skin the more certain she became that it probably wasn't even a real body at all. It had to be some sort of hoax. She held up a hand, one finger extended. "May I?"

Sheriff Mahon sighed and shook his head, but he handed her a glove. "Just don't disrupt anything." He held the edges of the bag apart so she could reach inside.

Under her gloved finger, the flesh of the corpse's shoulder gave like cold meat, which reminded her of her promise to find some flank steak for Katarina. She pressed a little harder and then, through the thin glove, she dug with her fingernail. When she took her hand away, it left no mark. The body was not sculpted of wax, which was the only thing, aside from it actually being Wes Edwards, that would have made sense.

Except, in Woodley, a lot of things made perfect sense even when they didn't make sense in the rest of the world.

"Listen, Sher... Dunn, I'm thinking."

He looked carefully at her for a moment before zipping the bag shut. "Why do I have a feeling I don't want to know what you're thinking?"

She let out a dry laugh of understanding. "Because I'm thinking this might be one of those things that only happens in Woodley. And I think you know what I mean."

Sheriff Dunn Mahon had been working for the county for decades, but he was still what people in Woodley referred to as "Not From Around Here." Cally could certainly empathize with that. Still, he'd been friends with the staff at Vale House long enough to have had a few experiences with the sort of thing she was talking about.

He remained silent as she followed him back around the

building. By the time they reached the door of the sheriff's office, wheels had begun turning in her head.

"I need you to trust me with something a little crazy," she said as they went back inside.

Resting his hands on the back of the desk chair, he closed his eyes and groaned softly. "What is it?" It almost wasn't a question.

"I need you to go ahead and sign Wes's car over to me."

"Well. Cally. I mean, Mr. Edwards would have to authorize that, first. Over the phone will be fine. We can call him. But you can't drive both your car and his back to the Yellow House. I really think you ought to bring him here to pick it up himself."

"Yes, except. What if that person in the Yellow House is not him?" Cally peered carefully into his face, but his eyes remained shut, as if he was trying to avoid seeing where her train of thought was going. "It's alright, Dunn. I don't need the car itself. All I need is the keys."

He opened his eyes at last, but shook his head. "Doesn't make any difference. Even if that body back there really is Wes Edwards, you're not his next of kin anymore so..."

"I promise to give them to Wes, or to his actual next of kin, tonight."

His shoulders sagged. "Alright, listen. I'll sign the keys into your temporary custody. But not the vehicle." He crossed the room and began rifling through one of the filing cabinets. "You'd better not get me brought up on malfeasance over this. Please get them back to me, or get him to come in and sign for them himself, by this time tomorrow at latest."

He drew a bulky brown envelope from the drawer and pushed aside enough clutter on his desk to make room for it. The envelope was printed with a column of blank lines labeled "Custodian." The sheriff crossed out his signature at the bottom of the list and handed the pen to Cally. After she signed and dated the line beneath his, he dumped out a ring of about half a dozen keys attached to a bottle-opener.

"Thanks, Dunn." She tucked them into her purse and pulled out her own car keys. "I promise, I'll let you know what I find out."

"I look forward to it," he said, not sounding like he was

looking forward to it at all. For the first time since she'd met him, Cally wanted to hug him.

The winter sun hung low over the parking lot, now, glaring into her eyes as she returned to the grid of busy streets. She had to hurry if she was going to get back to Woodley and do what she needed to do before it was time to meet Ben at the fence. But first, she remembered just as she was about to turn back onto the interstate, she had to stop at the GiantMart and pick up twelve pounds of flank steak.

14 – Cold Steel

Driving between the low, brick-fronted shops (many of which stood vacant) along both sides of Woodley's quiet Main Street, Cally wasn't sure what to do first, and that struck her as exceedingly odd. It had been a long time since her choices of what to do in such a tiny town were too numerous. She decided, as she drove past Dawes News, to combine two tasks by stopping there first.

She left her car idling at the curb and yanked mightily to heave open the shop's stubborn door. Ignoring Bree's glare over the top of her ubiquitous newspaper, she walked straight to the back of the store.

"I might be a little late tonight," she said as she came upon Ben cutting open bundles of the next day's newspapers. "Can you do me a huge favor and give this to Katarina when you head up that way?"

He accepted the heavy grocery bag she handed him, despite his bemused expression. "What is it?"

"It's for the tacos. You'll need to keep it in the cooler here until you clock out."

"Why can't you just...?"

She interrupted him with a quick peck on the lips. "I'll explain later. I have to hurry." She started to dash back to the front of the store, but Ben's patient grin stopped her in her tracks. Grinning, herself, though a bit sheepishly, she made herself pause long enough to give him a real kiss. "I'll see you in a little while," she promised, then ran back out to her car.

At the end of Main Street, instead of turning left to park in front of Vale House, she turned right and drove straight to the Yellow House. She put her own keys into her purse as she got out of the car, pulling out the set the sheriff had given her and carrying it with her to the house.

In the sullen shadows of dusk, she managed to avoid tripping over the ugly antique tree stand lurking at the top of the porch stairs. She recalled that Rosheen had told her she was welcome to just walk right into the house, but she hesitated anyway as she peered through the small, arched window in the door. She could smell food cooking, as always, and she could see a tiny antique porcelain Christmas tree glowing atop a half-moon table inside the entryway. The house's kitchen could be glimpsed at the far end of the hall, and from time to time she saw Brandon cross back and forth from stove to table. Wondering how many meals Brandon was cooking per day these days, she went in.

In the living room she could see a freshly cut pine tree, still tied with bailing twine, leaning against the corner beyond the sofa. Brandon came out of the kitchen with a peeled onion in one hand and gave her a quick, one-armed hug before he ushered her to the warm, cozily cluttered kitchen.

Rosheen was sitting at the old-fashioned wooden dinette table, entertaining her putative father-in-law with a story of her days playing bass in Brandon's band. Amid their laughter, Rosheen turned to wave Cally toward an empty chair. Brandon went back to the stove and began chopping the onion. It was the perfect, idyllic scene of the perfect little family get-together. Cally remained standing in the doorway.

"Callaghan!" What looked and sounded exactly like Wes Edwards stood up and offered his own chair to her. "Our son is making something with beans and tofu, but I won't be able to eat it. You may have my share."

"Oh, come on, Dad." Brandon dumped the onions into a large sauté pan. "Be brave. You might find out you like tofu."

"Right. Wes." Cally did not sit down. She did successfully prevent herself placing inflection quotes around the name "Wes" when she said it. "Remember what you always used to tell Brandon when he was afraid to try something new?"

He looked at her sidelong and laughed. "I told him...I told him it wasn't a good idea to eat something he wasn't used to."

"Your memory is a little off, I think." She bared her teeth in the semblance of a smile. Brandon began to grate ginger into the sizzling onions.

Wes's face grinned broadly. "It's just that I'm allergic."

"I see."

Claim of allergic reaction was the excuse Rosheen used to avoid handling iron or steel. Faeries couldn't come into contact with iron, Cally had read in many tales – the same tales in which she'd read about how, if a human ate faerie food, they would never be able to return to the human world. What would happen, she wondered, if a faerie ate human food?

"The fact is, I have somewhere I need to go." Wes, or whoever he was, nodded past Cally to the entryway behind her. "I'll get something to eat while I'm out."

"Do you need a lift? My car is just outside." Cally was unable to keep the edge out of her voice, that time, and the way his eyes flicked back to her showed he had noticed.

"Mom," Rosheen said conspiratorially. "I think he just wants to walk downtown by himself so he can buy something for Brandon and I for Christmas."

"Yes. Exactly." He lifted his chin, regarding Cally along the length of his nose, and then any remaining doubts in her mind evaporated. She'd seen that arrogant glare before. In fact she'd seen it on numerous faces, the first and last time she'd visited Faerie. Many of the fae people, particularly the Sluagh and the Fomorians, had looked at her that way. Including a certain Fomorian who had once impersonated another human she'd known, who had worn a dead man's face as a glamour in order to meddle in human affairs. That one had been incarcerated by the faerie queen for his deeds, but he'd had many loyal followers.

"It's a nice night for a walk." He stood and extended a hand to her. "Would you care to join me?"

Cally gripped the keys in her hand as if they were brass knuckles. "I just stopped by to give you these. The sheriff signed them over to me for you." She reached back to him, dropping the keys into his outstretched palm.

The sound he uttered when he jerked his hand back was

almost too high-pitched for Cally's ears to hear, but Rosheen apparently heard it. Her jaw dropped as she watched the keys hit the floor with a jangling crash. When the girl raised wide, green eyes to her, Cally nodded wordlessly at the understanding dawning in her face. Brandon, intent on the sizzling contents of his sauté pan, did not seem to have heard anything.

"Come to think of it," Cally said to the person who was using Wes's face to glare at her, "Thank you, yes. I think I will walk with you. We should talk." Stepping aside to clear the doorway, she turned and nodded to Rosheen. "Brandon can put the car keys in a safe place, for now."

Rosheen, eyes never leaving Cally's face, took a deep breath, swallowed, and nodded back.

The stranger dashed past Cally and headed for the door. Before she could spin around to follow, he had opened it and gone out. Cally groaned in frustration. Of course Brandon had made sure to change any steel doorknobs to brass ones the day he and Rosheen had moved in. She hurried out behind him, fearing he might already have run off into the night, but he had stopped at the top of the porch stairs and now turned back, smiling, to her.

"My beloved Callaghan," he began, laying a hand on her shoulder.

She made a point of not shrinking back, trying to gauge whether or not his hand felt as warm as a human's should. It did not, and she was too sure, now, to suppose this might just be an effect of the chilly air around them. She turned her face up as fearlessly as she could to look into his, but her voice still came out in a trembling whisper.

"Who are you?"

His eyes looked like Wes Edwards's had, as far as she could remember, but his smile was too patient and entirely too wide.

"Dearest Callaghan, you know who I am," he said gently. "I am the human who has always loved you. The one you once loved, and might love again one day."

Wes had never talked like that, and he had certainly never referred to people as "humans."

"Tell me who you are."

71

"Calla... Dear Cally. I am the ancestor of that unborn child in there." He turned and gazed back toward the door, and something about the earnestness in his voice, the expression on his face, made her think perhaps he wasn't lying about that part.

"Never mind, then." She brushed his hand off her shoulder. "It doesn't matter. What I really want to know is, what do you want with my family?"

"Want with them?" He laughed, not exactly like Wes had used to laugh, but not exactly unlike it, either. "I just want to be with them! To watch young Adam grow up, to be a part of his life. And I would love for you to be part of it, at my side. I think that would be *very* nice. We could be a nice, normal family, just like you always wanted." He gestured down the stairs into the deepening shadows along the road. "Come, you said you would walk with me. We can talk."

Following his gaze, she felt her stomach flip. "You know, I think I've changed my mind. I think I should just go on back inside now..."

"I mean you no harm. I was telling the truth when I said I would love to have you as my partner. Come with me." He reached a hand toward her but not, she noted, without flinching just a little.

She shook her head and did not reach back.

"Suit yourself, then." He turned away, looking into the deepening shadows along the road. "I do have errands to attend to, tonight, just as I said. I trust you'll still be joining us for dinner when Kelleigh arrives tomorrow night? Maybe we can talk then."

Giving the iron tree stand a wide berth, he ran lightly down the stairs, his feet on the wooden steps barely making a sound. When he reached the walkway, he did not turn toward Main Street, but disappeared in the opposite direction, walking swiftly south on Gardens Road.

The sky over the meadow was dark, though no stars were yet present. Cally thought Ben must already be waiting for her at the fence, but first she had to make sure everything was alright inside the house. She had to encourage Brandon to find the old steel doorknobs and put them back on the doors...

Rosheen met her in the entryway. Cally could see past her to where Brandon was now dumping chopped tomatoes into his pan, but Rosheen seized Cally by the elbow and led her into the living room. When they reached the farthest corner, she let go of Cally's arm and stood with her own arms stiff at her sides, staring at the bound evergreen tree.

"I always tell Brandon the truth." Rosheen's murmur was so soft, Cally had to lean close to listen. "I've told him everything about me. But what am I going to tell him about this?"

Cally couldn't understand the question. "We have to tell him the truth, of course. That that thing posing as his father is actually some kind of Sluagh or Fomorian or..."

"No!" Rosheen took one of Cally's hands and gripped it urgently. "I mean, yes, he's probably Fomorian. But I don't think he realizes you've seen through his glamour. We still have time..."

"I'm pretty sure I made it clear I no longer believe he's Wes." She looked out the window, toward the dark road where the stranger had disappeared. "But he didn't offer me any violence, so maybe you're right."

"They think humans are far less intelligent than fey kind," Rosheen said. "Generally, they're right. I think we should let him keep believing that, until we know what to do about him."

Cally looked through the doorway into the entry hall. She could hear Brandon getting silverware out of a drawer. "But you can't let that...that thing come back inside this house!"

"Shh!" Rosheen demonstrated by speaking quietly enough, herself, that her voice would not carry all the way to the kitchen. "Mom, I don't think he'll hurt us. He and his people, they've been looking for me all my life. You see? They just want to keep tabs on Adam's arrival. Don't worry, I have no illusions that their intentions are purely familial. Faeries don't have those kinds of feelings. But he won't hurt us."

Cally struggled to comply with Rosheen's wish for her to keep her voice down, but it made her whisper come out more like a hiss. "But he killed a man!"

Rosheen flinched as if Cally had struck her. "We don't know that!" she hissed back.

Watching the tears brimming in Rosheen's eyes, Cally

realized the young woman was not just talking about dealing with a Fomorian spy. She also desperately wanted not to have to tell Brandon his father might be dead. Cally had to admit she felt the same way.

Rosheen looked toward the kitchen, then back to Cally. "Under Rianwynn's rule," she explained urgently, "no faerie will dare intentionally shed human blood. Not even a Fomorian, except in fair battle. The price is too high. He couldn't have killed the real Wes. There has to be some other explanation."

"Rosheen I just... I don't think you're right. But I hope you are." Cally looked, also, through the doorway toward the kitchen. "Alright, I won't say anything to Brandon – not yet. I'll wait until I figure out what to do about *him*." She jerked her head toward the window. "But something has to be done!"

"We'll figure it out. We will. And in the meantime, please don't be worried about Brandon. I have his back. I'll keep him safe."

"Rosheen, I'm worried about you, too. And about the baby." And about whatever the darker tribes of the fae might actually be up to, now, but she didn't say that part.

"I'm starting to understand." Rosheen's eyes looked past Cally's face, past the window behind her and far beyond Gardens Road. "I should have listened when they told me not to go off in search of my father. If I had stayed where I was, stayed hidden, I wouldn't have met Brandon." She returned her gaze to Cally, reaching out to take both her hands. "I'm sorry. I should never have let myself get involved with him in the first place. But I was in love, and I didn't think through all the things that could happen. I'm so sorry."

Cally saw her own face, then, looking back at her from where Rosheen stood. She had said the same thing herself, on more than one occasion, about Ben.

"No." She shook her head and put her arms around the young woman. "No. Never, ever be sorry for falling in love with someone. We'll figure this out."

She turned away, wiping her eyes with her sleeve, and went back to the front door. "Tell Brandon I'm sorry I couldn't stay for supper, but there was something I had to do." She didn't know what she was actually going to do, but it would probably have something to do with marching into Faerie, herself, for help.

15 – The Crescent Moon

She was too late. For the first time since she had begun meeting Ben at the fence at nightfall, she got there too late to see him off. Few stars were visible in the sky, mainly because of the increasing cloud cover, but he had already left. She had run all the way to the fence in front of Vale House, and now she stood with her hands on the top rail, out of breath and sick with herself.

She knew he'd understand. He was not a petty man. It had to happen sometime, after all. And she had warned him she might be late – though she hadn't thought she'd be this late.

But her timing could not have been worse. She had come here planning, for the first time ever, to accept his perpetually open invitation to take her with him into Faerie. She gazed across the dark meadow, wondering if she might be able to find the way by herself. It wasn't likely. She'd been learning to follow the invisible faerie roads around Woodley, but she'd never yet made it all the way to Rianwynn's court. She cast her eyes south and north, hoping to catch a glimpse of one of the three horses who weren't really horses. They did know the way, and might be cajoled into carrying her there. But she was alone. She saw nothing moving in the cold, dark hills...

No. She did see a figure, a tall shadow, standing beside the fence just a short distance down the slope. Her heart leapt into her mouth – maybe she hadn't missed Ben after all! Maybe, by some miracle, he was still there waiting for her. But as the shadow began walking toward her she knew, by its movement and the sound of its footfalls through the dry grass, it wasn't him. She took her hands off the fence and shrank backward, trying to calculate, without turning to look, how many running steps it would take to get her safely to the Vale House front door.

"Cally." The voice whispered gently, and all the tension

melted out of her so quickly her knees nearly folded. She put her hands back on the fence to steady herself.

"Michael. You scared the hell out of me!"

He closed the distance between them and laid his hands on top of hers. "There has never been any hell in you, Callaghan McCarthy."

"You'd be surprised," she said, but she wanted to hug him. "It's good to see you."

"I came to give you your Christmas present early," he said. "As you may or may not already understand, I won't be able to attend the party."

Michael Dawes was Ben's and Bree's father. Though he was fully human, he was unable to return ever again from Faerie. He had given up much in his pursuit of Ben's mother, including the esteem of his own children. For this reason, Cally had still never got up the nerve to tell Ben about having met Michael, on a night quite different from this one, out in the hills during a previous unsuccessful attempt to untangle the paths leading to Faerie.

"Oh, Michael! I'm sure there's some way we can bend the rules to allow you to cross the fence, even if only for one night of the year.

"But I'm afraid there's a different reason I'm glad to see you tonight. I need to speak to the queen. There's something going on here she really ought to know about."

He picked up her hands and placed them palm-to-palm. The way he looked at her reminded her very much of Ben. The lines creasing his face were much deeper, his hair was streaked with wider swaths of gray, but his eyes were the same unusual shade of china blue. "You know I would do anything for you," he said, "if I could. But if this is about Eladha..."

She stepped back, pulling her hands out of his. "Eladha? No, why? I thought he was locked up in some faerie prison somewhere." Despite her words, she turned to look toward Gardens Road.

Michael shook his head. "No faerie ever stays incarcerated forever. And Eladha is clever. He found a loophole some weeks ago, and disappeared from the Sidhe's sight. Queen Rianwynn has been more than a little agitated about this, as you can imagine."

"Not as agitated as I am," Cally thought, squinting into the Christmas lights around the porch of the Yellow House. "It can't be him. Eladha wouldn't have just let me walk away." She tore her gaze from the lights and looked back at Michael. "But it could be one of his, I don't know, pawns or foot soldiers or whatever he calls them. Let's go." She bent to duck under the top fence rail.

"Woah, woah!" Even Michael's laugh reminded her of Ben's. "It's alright – you don't have to go anywhere. I'll get word to her for you."

"How are you going to do that? She no longer allows you in her presence."

"But she tolerates Ana." Ana was Ben's other daughter, a wild fae woman who was currently living at Rianwynn's court. "And Ana is happy enough to talk to me, if only because it annoys Rianwynn so much. We'll take care of everything on our end. You need to stay here."

Cally had to admit, she did feel a lot better about remaining nearby, knowing that whoever was posing as Wes intended to return to the Yellow House.

"Alright, Michael. I'll count on you to get word to the queen for me." She leaned across the fence to kiss his cheek. His ungroomed beard was rougher and scratchier than Ben's.

"Cally – wait." He caught her hand before she could turn back to Vale House. "Have you made your wish yet?"

She sighed in exasperation. "That's *so* not important right now!" Her voice came out much sharper than she meant it to.

"It's just..." He reached his free hand into his jacket, groping for something inside it. "I thought, if you and Ben might happen to make the same wish. Well. You know. It could come true."

Cally paused, considering his words. Would Ben, would he ever, make the same wish she would make if she had the heart to?

"You can't make a wish that interferes with someone's free will," Michael reminded her. "So you can't wish for him to stay here in the human world with you, and he can't wish for you to join him on this side of the fence. But if you and he both made the same wish, then neither of you would be interfering with the other's free will."

"All we'd have to do is agree which side of the fence to live on."

"And therein lies the rub. Because if you did that, you'd be telling one another what your wish is, and that would cause it not to come true."

A number of choice words went through Cally's head describing faerie magic and its convoluted rules, but she kept them to herself. "So there you are," she said. "This is why I'm wary of wishing. There's always something. The other shoe always drops, and then..."

He turned her hand palm up. Removing his other hand from inside his jacket, he pressed something into her fingers. It felt like a small, round object, warm from having been next to his body, and as he took his hand away she saw a silver chain spilling over her palm. "I just thought this might help."

She held the pendant up to the intermittent moonlight. It was the silver crescent, with a flat crystal suspended between its points, that he'd demonstrated to her once before. He'd shown her how one could look through the crystal to see through faerie glamour, to see things as they truly were.

"Michael, you can't give me this!"

"I can," he said. "You're the Armadeur of this Vale, now, whether you believe it or not. Anyway I don't need it anymore. But I have a feeling you'll be able to make good use of it. Merry Christmas!" He bowed slightly and turned away, but then paused and turned back. "Oh, and next time you're in the presence of faeries, even Queen Rianwynn herself, try using it to look at their feet."

"Their feet?"

But he swiftly slipped away into the shadows, possibly because someone else had come through the masonry gate from Main Street and was walking across the lawn toward her.

10 – A Candle in the Window

She thought the hunched figure limping toward her was Rum, at first, but whoever it was wasn't quite short enough to be the ancient land wight. It was not until the person spoke that Cally realized who it was.

"You were supposed to come back to the store tonight to talk to me!"

"Oh! God, Bree, I'm so sorry. I completely forgot. So much has happened today..." It was all she could do not to run forward to support the old woman by the elbow, the way Ben would have done, but she had a feeling only he could get away with that sort of expression of tenderness toward his sister.

"Yeah, I figured." Bree closed the last few steps between them. "Never snows but it's a blizzard, around here."

"You don't mean that literally, do you?" Cally looked at Bree out of the side of one eye, then glanced at the sky. The ragged clouds of the night before were clumping together now into larger masses, limned around their edges by the nearly full moon, but she didn't think they looked particularly stormy. "Sorry, I guess we can go back and have our talk now. I'll help you close up shop." She turned toward the gateway from which Bree had just emerged, but the old woman was headed in the opposite direction.

"Already done," she said over her shoulder as she stumped along the fence. "Not much business tonight anyway. Would you like to walk me home?" It wasn't a question.

"What? Sure, I mean..." As far as Cally knew, Bree had always walked home alone before. "I guess I can do that." She turned around and followed her down the slope of the lawn. Despite her limp, Bree seemed to negotiate the terrain well enough.

Neither of them spoke as they passed the barn and

approached the bottom of the Vale House grounds. Here, the old farm pond filled the hollow before the rise up to Bells Road. In the faint moonlight, its surface gleamed softly between bare willow and river birch branches. A jagged shelf of ice, less than a foot wide in places, rimmed the shallow edges of the pond, especially around the wooden pier on the western side, but for the most part black, open water reflected the clouds above.

Cally wanted to stop, here, to contemplate how a grown man could have drowned (or been drowned) in that pond, as well as the mystery of how Ian's fishing boat had both disappeared from this landlocked dock and was, by all accounts, due to reappear here any moment. The old woman gave the dark water not a glance, however. Without pausing she continued, in her wobbly but determined stride, right on around the bank to the open field on the far side.

The ground sloped gently back up again until it reached the railroad embankment which bisected the field between Bells Road and Woodley proper. Cally caught up with Bree, forgetting not to reach out and grasp her arm to steady her as they stepped across the tracks. Bree made no complaint, but continued onward to the unmarked stretch of blacktop.

The road was lined on its far side with modest cottages, some with picket fences, all facing away from the forest behind them. Most of them were fairly modern. All of them had at least one friendly light glowing in a front window, and many of them were heavily decorated with Christmas lights. The cottage toward which Bree now turned, at the easternmost end of the road before it dead-ended at the meadow fence, was not decorated, though a single electric candle did burn in one window.

"This is one of the original cottages!" Cally realized as Bree lurched up onto the flat porch and crossed to the door. "One of the ones that were here before Ian developed the rest of the street, right?"

"This is, in fact, *the* original cottage," Bree corrected.

Cally expected the old woman to pause and fumble in her purse for keys. Instead, she simply turned the knob and opened the door.

"Bree, you shouldn't leave your house unlocked. Especially

since you live alone!"

"Nobody is going to mess with my home." The look she threw over her shoulder, as she stepped inside and switched on a lamp, inclined Cally to agree. She could all too easily recall a different side of Bree – one nobody in their right mind would ever want to cross.

"Coffee?" The old woman took off her coat and threw it over the back of an armchair.

"Thanks, but no. It's a little late for coffee, for me." Cally looked around the room which, while cluttered with little tables and overstuffed furniture, managed to look like nobody lived in it.

Bree stumped through a doorway into what turned out, when she switched on the overhead light, to be the kitchen. Cally crossed to the boarded-up fireplace on the opposite side of the room. Atop the mantelpiece a row of framed photographs, interspersed with vases of dried roses and baby's-breath, stretched from end to end. All of it was covered with a soft layer of cobwebs and dust. All except for one photo...

"So Bree, be honest," Cally called into the kitchen. "Did you write that story? The one on the floppy?" She picked up the single frame that had been carefully cleaned and polished.

"As a famous author," Bree called back, "you probably think it's pretty lousy writing."

"I'm not famous. And no, it's not bad writing at all, for a first draft. Kind of enchanting, actually. Did you write it?"

The frame held a yellowed black-and-white photograph of a dark-haired youth, about fifteen years old, standing beside a vintage sports car with his arm around a little girl who was sitting on the car's roof. Both of them wore wide grins, and Cally did not need for the picture to be in color to know they both had brilliant, china-blue eyes.

This cottage had once, she realized, also been Ben's home. Her eyes scanned the small space, settling on a narrow hallway leading to rooms at the back of the house. One of those rooms would have been Ben's childhood bedroom. She imagined him gazing into the forest outside his window every night, watching his mother slipping away into Faerie, always to return by morning, except for that one, last time...

"I wrote it a long time ago." This time Bree's voice came from near her elbow. "I never finished it."

Cally gently put the photo back in its place.

"Why didn't you finish it?"

"I moved on." Bree had brought two cups of coffee, one of which she handed to Cally before Cally could remind her that she didn't want any.

She accepted the cup anyway. "I understand. I moved on from my own writing several times. Unfortunately, my muse refused to agree to the divorce." Bree, still standing, took a deep gulp of her own coffee. By way of avoiding following suit, Cally asked, "So who is Emerald?"

"She's a character in a story, of course." The old woman looked over the brim of her cup with the "duh!" so clear in her eyes she didn't have to say it out loud.

"But she's more than that," Cally had to insist. "She's my friend. I've been talking to her for years."

"Have you ever met her?" Bree still did not sit down or offer Cally a seat. "In real life?"

"Well. No. But we have long conversations. She has a personality. She's clearly not just an internet bot, or a character with no will of her own. And Bree, I know you know that. You want to know what I know about her, just as much as I want to know what you know. That's why you gave me the disk in the first place."

She took a reluctant sip of coffee and moved toward the sofa. The brew was every bit as bitter as the stuff that sat on the burner for hours every day at the news store, but in order to get answers, Cally was willing to sit down and try to drink it.

"What does she look like?" Bree asked as she turned around and went back into the kitchen. Cally could hear cupboards opening and shutting. Sighing, she set her cup down on one of the end tables and followed. The overhead light in the little kitchen was too bright for the small space; it made everything in the room look hard and cold.

"I don't know what she looks like, Bree. I was hoping you could tell me. After all, *you* created her."

Bree stopped opening and shutting cupboards. She had not, as far as Cally could tell, taken anything out of or put anything into any of them.

"What do you mean by that?" she demanded, her back still to Cally. Cally felt a sudden unease come over her, a crawling chill in the pit of her stomach that had nothing to do with the wretched coffee. It was as if Bree was staring at her without even having to turn around.

"I mean. Well, it's perfectly alright, of course." Cally had often, herself, postponed coming up with physical descriptions of her characters until she got to know them better. But she didn't really want to get drawn into a writerly discussion about character creation. She had questions that needed answering.

Bree opened a drawer and banged it shut again.

Cally took a deep breath. "I have a theory," she offered. "Well, barely a hypothesis, really. But if anyone would know, it would be you. Is this all, I don't know, some kind of artifact of the magic of this Vale?" Cally gestured with both arms, indicating everything around the little cottage on Bells Road. "Book characters come to life here, or something?" It occurred to her that maybe she should start being more careful what kinds of characters she created, now that she lived here.

When Bree turned around, her expression was no longer stony. It was now so full of so many emotions, from anger to sorrow to disgust, that all of them seemed to seethe like snakes just beneath the surface of her skin. Her hands were trembling visibly. "I think you need to go now," she said in a low growl.

Cally found herself agreeing wholeheartedly. Holding her breath, she walked backwards as Bree followed her, step by step, into the cottage living room. She didn't want to move too suddenly, but if Bree should begin to transform into...whatever it was she had transformed into, that time... She moved sideways until her outstretched hand encountered the door. She opened it slowly, and the cold air rushing in from outside helped her find her breath again.

As she stepped over the threshold, wondering if she should turn and run or if it would be safer to just continue walking backwards, she thought she saw the old woman's face suddenly soften. Maybe it was just a trick of the way the light from the kitchen flowed over her shoulder, but only the sorrowful parts of her expression remained. Cally really didn't want to stand there one second longer, but she felt suddenly moved to answer Bree's question after all.

"I have always pictured her as tall," she said. "Taller than I am, anyway. With dark hair, wavy, down to about here." She held a hand out beside her own hip. "I'm not sure what color her eyes are. For some reason, even though her name is Emerald, I have always imagined them to be more of an amethyst shade."

Bree nodded past Cally's shoulder into the night.

"Yes," she said. "That sounds about right." Then she reached out and softly shut the door in Cally's face.

17 – Thirteen Hours

C ally...I'm sorry to wake you."

Ben was leaning over the bed, gently shaking her by the shoulder. Tarnish-colored light filled the room behind him.

"No, I like it when you wake me." She sat up a little too quickly, making her head spin. She lay back down and lifted the covers beside her, inviting him to join her. "What time is it?"

Instead of looking at the bedside clock, he looked out the window. "About twenty past seven." He did not lie down beside her but reached toward the bedside chair where she'd thrown her clothes the night before. Handing a wrinkled blouse to her, he said, "The sheriff is downstairs. He says he needs to talk to you."

Cally said an unladylike word and sat up on the edge of the bed. Reaching out to accept the blouse, she said, "I'm sorry I missed you at the fence last night. I really needed to talk to you. Did you hear what happened?"

"It's okay." He looked away as she stood up and skinned out of her nightgown, but she was too distracted, speculating about the news the sheriff might have brought, to wonder why he would do this. "We can talk later," he said.

As she unfurled the blouse to put it on, something fell from between its folds. She gasped, realizing what it was before it hit the dogwood-blossom rug. It was the crescent-moon pendant Michael had given to her – she'd forgotten all about it. She glanced quickly up at Ben, but he was still studying the back of the door. Before he could turn around, she stooped and picked the amulet up. She knew she had to talk to him eventually about having met his father, but today didn't seem like a good time. No day ever really seemed like a good time to bring up her acquaintance with the man against whom

Ben still held what was probably the only grudge he'd ever held.

She grabbed her jeans from the back of the chair and slipped the pendant into the pocket as she put them on. Her stealth was unnecessary; Ben did not look back at her until she said, "Alright. Ready." She wondered why he was being so prudish. They were well past the chastely-averted-eyes stage of their relationship.

"He's on the porch," Ben explained, opening the bedroom door and holding it for her. "I think he's hoping to avoid kitchen table talk with the rest of the household."

No ghosts were present at the gallery railing or in the Hall as they descended the stairs, but Bethany was haunting the switchboard. As Cally passed the desk, she noticed two full mugs of coffee beside the phone.

"Are those for us?" she asked hopefully.

Bethany stood, picking up one of the mugs. "Oh, no, sorry. This one's for Dunn." She started toward the front door where Cally could see, through the glass oval, the silhouette of a man at the porch railing.

"It's alright, Bethany." Cally deftly swooped the mug out of the older woman's hand. "I'll take it to him."

Bethany didn't miss a beat. "I'll get two more cups from the kitchen, then," she said, "and bring them out to you and Ben."

It was Ben who smiled and laid a gentle hand on Bethany's shoulder. "That won't be necessary," he said. "I'm heading straight in to the store this morning."

Cally thought that was odd, but he didn't pause to explain. Kissing her swiftly on the cheek, he opened the door and went out onto the porch. She heard the two men briefly exchanging polite remarks as Ben hurried down the stairs. Lifting an eyebrow, she turned to look at Bethany.

Bethany had noticed it, too. "He's acting awfully strange this morning."

All Cally could do was nod. Surely he couldn't be angry about her having been late the night before?

"Bethany, please phone the kitchen extension and tell Katarina I'll be in for breakfast shortly."

Bethany let out a snort and subsided back to her station

behind the desk while Cally carried the sheriff's coffee out to him.

Ben had already disappeared around the side of the house. Sheriff Mahon was leaning against the porch railing, squinting at the sky above the meadow. The rising sun warmed some of the gray horizon to the east but, for the most part, a lumpy blanket of steel-colored clouds roiled unbroken from horizon to horizon. Cally thought they truly did look, as far as she could recall, like the type of clouds that could produce snow, or at least sleet. The three horses – black, white, and chestnut – seemed unconcerned as they grazed quietly a few yards beyond the fence.

Handing the sheriff's coffee to him, she said, "Careful. It's hot."

"Thanks, Ms. Mc... Cally." He took a deep, slurping sip and then turned to face her. "It's starting to look like I might owe you an apology."

He gestured with his free hand toward one of the wicker chairs beside the door, but Doctor Boojums was curled up in it, pretending to be asleep. Cally leaned against the railing beside the sheriff instead.

"I've received some preliminary fingerprint data," he went on. "Turns out, the prints on that car and its contents were all from one person. Whoever it was apparently has no criminal record, as there's no name attached to them. But the prints did match the body from the pond. It's starting to look like our John Doe might really be Wesley Edwards, after all, and that whoever is in that house..." he jerked his head toward Gardens Road, "has taken Mr. Edwards's wallet and is impersonating him."

He paused to give her, she imagined, a chance to say something like "I tried to tell you!" but a different thought had found its way to the front of her mind.

"Dunn... I just have one question for you. Do you ever sleep?"

He laughed loudly enough that the horses in the meadow all picked up their heads and swiveled their ears toward him. Then he said, "This is the part where you tell me who *you* think the man in the Yellow House is."

"You don't want to hear it."

"Try me." He set the coffee mug down on the railing. "I used to get all resentful that nobody in this town would talk to me about... you know. This sort of stuff. Now that they're becoming more willing to open up, I find myself reluctant to listen. So go ahead. Push me out of my comfort zone, here, Cally. I trust you."

She was moved that he would say this, but her attention kept drifting from the meadow to the intersection with Gardens Road and back again. "It's just the usual story," she said. "Fomorians trying to reclaim what they feel is rightfully theirs: lordship over the kingdoms of Faerie. Sometimes using human pawns to accomplish their goals. In this case I think they're hoping to infiltrate..."

She hesitated. She didn't know if it would be right to tell him about Rosheen not being anywhere near as human as she looked. That was Rosheen's own story to tell, and she hadn't even told all of it to Cally, yet.

"Fomorians?" the sheriff asked.

"Bad faeries. Nutshell version."

"Hmph." He turned to gaze once more toward the golden light pushing its way up from the horizon beneath the cloud cover. While his expression remained unreadable, it wasn't one of disbelief, and he made no attempt to inform Cally she was out of her mind.

At length he said, "Alright. Now, if that was really what's going on here, how would you recommend we proceed?"

"I've got messengers out, working on that for me."

"Of course you do." His voice was utterly flat. He took another deep gulp of coffee, and when he set the cup back on the railing, it was nearly empty. "Any idea when they'll get back to you?"

"Do you need me to put some brandy in that?" She nodded toward the coffee cup.

That got a smile out of him. She did her best to answer his question. "Most of them won't get back to me until after sunset. I mean, they won't come here in the daytime. But there is one person I can talk to."

"You mean Ben Dawes."

"What do you know about him?"

92

"Well, everyone in this town seems to take it for granted there's something off about him," said the sheriff. "Not in a bad way, or anything. But I hear people say things sometimes, just offhand, that make it seem like he's been around a lot longer than he actually could have been. I mean, if some of the stories people tell about him were true, he'd have to be a hundred years old by now."

Cally carefully did not look at him. "Not quite."

He shook his head. "I'm pretty sure he's not one of those stalkery vampires, anyway. No, I don't expect you to spill his story to me. That wouldn't be right. I'll buy him a drink sometime and see if he'll tell me himself."

"You might need to take up day-drinking for that." Cally did turn to meet his eyes, then. "I need to, um, run a few errands. Important ones. Where are you off to next?"

"I was planning to go back to the Yellow House and confront this fellow who claims to be Wes Edwards."

"Sheriff. Dunn. Would you...Please? Give me a little more time before you do that? This needs to be handled with some delicacy to prevent..." She wasn't sure what would happen if someone tried to arrest whoever the faerie entity was. If the sheriff tried to put steel handcuffs around a Fomorian's wrists, the situation could escalate from tense to explosive. Sheriff Mahon could be badly hurt or, if he felt forced to draw his gun, it could ignite a full-blown Human/Faerie war. "Can you give me just, say, ten more hours? Twelve, to be safe."

She met his eyes as squarely as she could. He might not have been a lifelong resident of Woodley, but he was clearly a veteran of law-enforcement and she could feel his gaze going through and through her, assessing and measuring everything from her expression to her breathing to the dilation of her pupils.

He let out a long breath and released her from his stare. "The old-guard around here seems to put great stock in you," he said at last. "Even though you're greener than I am. I'm going to go ahead and run with that." He picked up his coffee cup. "This investigation has generated a lot of paperwork I need to attend to. And when they finally get back to me with those dental records, I'll have to include my conclusions about them in my report, too. Standard bureaucratic bull...due diligence, and all. I'm afraid all this might take at least thirteen hours."

Cally gave him a quick, one-armed hug. "Thanks, Dunn. I promise I won't let you down." She hoped she wasn't making a promise she couldn't keep.

He peered into the dregs of his coffee, then carried it to the front door. "I think I need a refill," he said.

18 – Further Instructions

While the sheriff waited in the Hall, doing an impressive job of filling Bethany in without actually telling her anything, Cally carried the empty mug to the kitchen. This time, the sight of the work table and the window over the sink failed to fill her with the usual warm emotions and memories. She hurried to the coffee maker on the counter, trying to think of some way to avoid having to explain why Ben would not be joining them for breakfast today.

Katarina had placed a toaster oven and a selection of breakfast-sandwich ingredients on the counter, as most of the work table was covered with mixing bowls and bags of flour. "Today is tortilla-making day!" she announced cheerfully, donning an apron with a Christmas tree appliqué on its bib. "Also! Ignacio says he believes Ian and Sofie will arrive today! He's down by the pond right now, clearing the ice so they don't slip when they get out of the boat. I need to get cracking so I'll have time to sit down and talk with them later when they...what's the matter?"

Cally had refilled the sheriff's cup, but now she stood motionless with it in her hand, staring through the window toward the little white gate at the rear of the yard. A quiet stretch of Main Street, just visible through the bare crape myrtle branches, was slowly filling with what daylight there would be today.

"And where's Ben?" Katarina went on. "You two haven't had a fight, have you?"

Cally turned around. "Honestly, Kat, I don't know. I guess I'd better go find out. Can you give this to the sheriff for me?"

Without waiting for a reply, she set the mug down and went out the back door. She tried not to hurry through the residential section – the residents already had enough to gossip about, these

95

days. As she reached the beginning of downtown, she could see Brandon coming out of the news store. He waved when he spotted her.

"Yo, Mom!" He let the door swing shut behind him. "Ben came in early today and told me to take the rest of the day off. I didn't try very hard to turn down his offer!" He closed the distance between them and gave her a hug.

Turning around, he smiled over his shoulder through the store's display window, through which they could both see Ben's back. He seemed to be talking animatedly to someone in the rear of the store. "Isn't he awesome?"

"He is," Cally said, hoping Brandon wouldn't notice the tension in her voice. "Did your...dad, get back to your house okay last night?"

"He got back really late. Closer to morning, to be honest. But yes, he's back now. Upstairs sleeping off whatever he was up to all night! Guess he'll never change, will he?" Brandon shook his head, but he was still smiling.

Unable to think of what to say to that, Cally settled on: "Well, you never know." She wanted to tell her son to be careful, but she didn't want to have to explain what he should be careful of. That ball was in Rosheen's court, at the moment.

As Brandon, waving, turned away, Cally tugged on the shop door handle. The door stuck, as always, so she braced her feet against the step and tugged harder. It still wouldn't open. She swore under her breath. She swore out loud. It was just one more thing she was in no mood to deal with this morning. Glaring at the door as if it were to blame for everything that had ever gone wrong in her entire life, she balled up her fist as if to punch the stupid inanimate object. She knew it would hurt her a lot more than it would hurt the door, but Ben's appearance on the other side saved her having to make that decision.

He was smiling, as always. He kicked the door from the inside, just as he had done on the first morning she'd met him and, when it shuddered open, he leaned out still smiling. He shut the door softly after she entered, and then she didn't know what to do. She didn't know what to say – she didn't even know what was wrong.

96

Afraid she might start sobbing any second, she put her arms around him and buried her face in his chest.

"Hey," was all he said, quietly into the hair over her ear.

Behind her, she heard Bree clear her throat. She heard the rustle of newspaper pages flipping. She felt Ben chuckle silently as he turned away and, taking her by the hand, led her to the back of the store.

An absolutely stunning brunette woman was standing there watching them both. When Cally and Ben got close enough, the woman slipped an arm around Ben and smiled brilliantly into Cally's face. "Hullo, Stepmom," she said.

"Don't call me that." If Cally had been in a better mood, she might have said something more diplomatic. She had tried to get along with Ben's eldest but, unlike Rosheen, there was something about Ana's demeanor that always made Cally feel like a mouse in the claws of a particularly playful cat.

Ana laughed, a lovely, musical laugh from perfect, pouty red lips. "I guess you're right!" she said. "After all, you and Dad aren't married!"

Cally knew this was meant to be a passive-aggressive jab, but she suddenly realized why Ana was there. "Do you have some news for me?" she asked. "Or instructions, maybe?"

"I do." Ana looked sideways at Cally from under her lashes. "But perhaps you don't want me to talk about that in front of Auntie." She nudged Ben's shoulder with her own. "Or in front of this guy."

"What? Why would I not... Oh. You're referring to Mi... my messenger."

Ana's smile was that of a mischievous child who had been told not to touch something and was on the point of doing so anyway, just to prove she could.

Ben looked back and forth from Cally to Ana, clearly not understanding what was going on between them, waiting to be included in the conversation. Cally did her best to explain to him without explaining too much. "It was me who sent word to Rianwynn," she said. "I found out about it during my visit to the Yellow House. That was why I was too late to meet you at the fence."

She wished they were alone so she could seek a little temporary comfort in his arms. His patient gaze was reassuring, at least, so she went on. "Anyway after I sent word to the queen..." It suddenly occurred to her that maybe he had figured out who the messenger was. Maybe that was why he had been acting so distant this morning. She would have to deal with that later. "I was expecting information or instructions this morning. I thought you might bring them, but I guess they gave that job to Ana."

He drew his brows together and shook his head, but Ana spoke up before he could ask for clarification. "Daddy wasn't there. He was wandering around in the shadows, moping about something. He never does seem to appreciate the party atmosphere in Grandma's court."

Ben seemed to want to say something in defense of himself, but Ana stepped between him and Cally. "So here are your instructions," she continued. "You are to do nothing. You are to wait until nightfall. The Queen and her select warriors will be waiting outside the gate. Maybe I'll come along, too! You are to open the gate for us."

"And then..?"

"That's all I got for you. Maybe you'll get some further instructions then!" Ana's grin flashed perfect, white teeth behind ruby lips, but to Cally it seemed like the woman was baring fangs dripping with venom. If she ever got a chance, she thought, she really must look at this faerie/human woman through the amulet Michael had given her.

Ana turned and gave Ben a peck on the cheek, then spun on her stiletto heels and headed for the front of the store. "Later, Auntie!" she called as she clattered past Bree at the counter. Bree did not look up from her paper. The bell above the door jangled when Ana opened it effortlessly, but Cally didn't see her cross in front of the display window after she went outside.

Behind her, Ben let out a breath that was, for him, the closest thing Cally had ever heard to exasperation. "*What* was all that about?"

She turned with a genuinely sympathetic smile. "She has that effect on you, too, I see?"

His expression did soften a little, but his eyes were still serious, his hand still outstretched toward the spot Ana had so hastily vacated. He turned it toward Cally, instead, and spoke her thoughts aloud before she could voice them herself.

"Can we talk?"

19 – Different Stories

T he only vehicles in the gravel lot behind the store were the Dawes family Daimler, and Ennilangr's eighteen-wheeler with its mural of leaping rams on the trailer. The delivery driver himself was nowhere in sight. Ben drew Cally to the antique sports car and sat down on its hood. She didn't make any arguments, this time, about marring the paint.

"Listen, I'm sorry about last night!" she blurted as she sat down beside him. "But..."

"Hey!" He took one of her hands, holding it against his thigh like he thought it might try to escape. Turning to look into her eyes, he said, "It's alright! I understand. You need to be with your family. I don't want to be in the way."

"But you didn't hear what happened!" She shuddered. "I've been losing my mind about it all night long!"

"I was there. I did hear. I keep trying to tell you, I understand. I know this must be hard on your heart, but you don't need to lose your mind over it."

"I don't need to...?" She couldn't believe he could be so cavalier about the presence of a Fomorian spy in Woodley. "Ben, this is serious!"

"Of course it is." He nodded, and his expression was indeed serious. "Just know that whatever you decide, I'll support you. I only want what's best for you."

"Whatever *I* decide?" She was pretty sure this was the kind of decision only the Queen of Faerie had the authority to make.

His grip on her hand had grown quite firm. He inhaled deeply, nodding, and let go of it. Cally could swear she saw tears forming in the corners of his eyes, and that made her wonder if she had in fact lost her mind somewhere between last night and this

100

morning.

He swallowed, struggling to control his voice which came out, now, just above a whisper. "You have a right to be confused. I could hear the passion in Wes's voice. He still loves you, and who could blame him? He's offering you a normal life, and..."

"Oh, my god!" Cally slid off the hood and stood up. "You were there? You heard that?"

"I didn't mean to intrude on your privacy." His hands curled into fists as he looked down at them in his lap. "Katarina told me you weren't home, so I knew you must be at the Yellow House. I went to wait for you at the fence on the other side of Gardens Road, and I overheard what should have been a private conversation. I'm sorry. I just want you to know: I will never stand in the way of your happiness..."

"No!" She didn't know whether to laugh or cry. She flung herself into his lap, wrapping both arms and legs around him, unconcerned now that their combined weight was definitely denting the hood of the Daimler. "I think we're talking about two different things," she said. "That man... that *person* I was talking to on the porch of the Yellow House last night, that was not Wes Edwards!"

She pulled herself back enough to make sure he could see her face. His expression, still patient and sorrowful, was now also clouded with incomprehension. She hurried to clarify. "I don't know who it was. Someone from Faerie. A Sluagh or a Fomorian. I sent someone to speak to Rianwynn about it."

His smile did not yet return, but he threw his head back and drew in a deep breath. As he let it out slowly, his shoulders sank and Cally could feel the tension melting out of his body. "I'm sorry," he said at length, shaking his head. "I'm so sorry. I completely misunderstood."

She was sorry, too, that he had apparently gone all night and morning thinking he was in danger of losing her. Losing her sooner than they were expecting, anyway.

"Ana wasn't lying," he went on. "When your message was brought to Rianwynn, I didn't hear about it. I spent my obligatory night in Faerie pacing back and forth in the shadows of the courtyard, feeling sorry for myself. Mustering the courage to assure you I only want you to be happy, should you choose to return to a normal life."

Cally's own tension escaped from her in an abrupt laugh. "You dope!" She laid a hand on either side of his face. "I don't want a normal life! I want this life. This one I've found with you, in all its glorious weirdness."

And then her laughter faded as she raised her eyes to the tops of the surrounding buildings. Gazing eastward, toward where the Yellow House lay, she said, "Anyway, a normal life is the last thing he could offer me. Either one of him: the real Wes, or the..."

He disentangled her from around himself and slid off the car. "Now I'm doubly sorry," he said, following her gaze. "This really is important, and here I've been wallowing in my own little personal drama." Nodding, he took her hand. "Come on – we should get over there."

"There's nothing we can do right now. It's like Ana said: the queen will come tonight and handle it. Until then we're to..."

"Is that why your next stop, after you left here, was going to be the Yellow House?" He gave her a sidelong smile.

She had to confess. "I have never been very good at not doing what I shouldn't do."

His expression sobered again. "Cally. I know you don't need protecting. It's not that. I just want to see for myself. I want to see that Rosheen is alright. Bree," he concluded with a swift nod toward the rear wall of the news store, "will just have to manage without anyone to boss around for a little while."

She let him lead her to the gap between the store and the vacant shop beside it. "It's just," she said, fighting her urge to pull backwards on his hand, "I'm not sure what I plan to do once I get there."

"I'm not sure, either." He drew her along the alleyway toward the stretch of Main Street that could be glimpsed between the buildings. "There's only one thing I'm ever sure about, these days." He stopped abruptly. Pulling her against him, he said, "I love you."

What might have become a long and passionate kiss was interrupted by the sound of a car passing by outside the alley, headed toward the residential district with its radio blaring Christmas music. They turned to look, and Cally nodded her confirmation of what they both realized. "Kelleigh has arrived," she said. "I guess we'd better finish this later."

20 – Sládha

Rosheen seemed surprised to see Ben at her front door, but she reached out and drew him inside before Cally could even tell him not to bother knocking.

"I'm glad you finally get to see our home, Father!" She wrapped him in a warm hug, and Cally pondered how ironic it was that when Rosheen called him "Father" it sounded so much more affectionate than when Ana called him "Daddy."

A great pile of luggage and wrapped presents filled the entryway. Inside the living room, the Christmas tree had been erected next to the front window. Brandon and Gordon stood next to it with eggnog cups in hand, discussing the tree stand Brandon had engineered from a vintage produce crate filled with white pebbles. A young woman who looked like a younger and much more sophisticated version of Cally jumped up from the couch and crossed the room to throw her arms around Cally.

"O. M. G. Mom! This woman has managed to civilize my brother!" Kelleigh extended an arm to include Rosheen in the hug. "Did you ever think you'd see the day?" Then she stood back to smile at Ben. "And I'm pretty sure I've seen you, once before." She winked at Cally. "I had a feeling about the two of you, even back then."

Cally had never seen Ben blush, but she thought he looked like he might do so when Kelleigh hugged him, too.

"I'm glad to finally meet you formally," he said. "You look just like your mother."

"I take that as a very great compliment!" Laughing, she waved Gordon over to be introduced. Brandon gestured toward the old milk-glass eggnog bowl on the coffee table and told Ben to help himself. Cally couldn't tell whether Ben looked flustered because he was unaccustomed to being treated like part of an ordinary family, or if he was just distracted by other concerns as his eyes flitted around the room.

"Where's, um, your father?" he asked.

Kelleigh seemed to be wondering the same thing as she glanced back through the entryway to the foot of the stairs. "Brandon says he was out all night. Nice to know some people never change, eh?" Her tone and expression lost a good deal of their cheer at this, but she rapidly changed the subject. Waving everyone toward the Christmas tree, she said, "Come look at all this amazing stuff!" The tree had been covered with dozens of antique blown-glass ornaments from the attic. They glowed warmly amidst the branches and colored lights, though the tinsel garland (which had apparently once been some shade of lavender) had grown a bit sparse over the years. "I bet you could get a thousand bucks for these things on eMarket!" Kelleigh gushed.

Cally sought out and caught Rosheen's eye. *What are we going to do?* She wanted to scream. *What the hell are we going to tell them?* She didn't scream, or even speak, but she knew Rosheen knew exactly what she was thinking.

She was almost tempted to let whoever was sleeping upstairs just go ahead and keep up their charade, take Wes's place and make this look like the nearly-normal family Kelleigh and Brandon believed it was finally becoming. She was unable to convince herself, though, that this scenario could ever end in anything but disaster.

Brandon turned away from the tree. "Let me show you guys your room," he said to his sister. He and Gordon headed out into the entryway and began collecting luggage. Cally picked up two small cases and followed them up the stairs.

"Be quiet, you guys," Rosheen called softly. "Try not to wake our other guest."

Brandon laughed. "I'm actually hoping Dad will hear us trooping up and down the hall and decide it's time for some strong coffee!" He set a suitcase down next to the first doorway past the top of the stairs. Gesturing his sister and brother-in-law toward it with a bow, he turned to wink at Cally. "Mom, our house is becoming almost as much a Bed and Breakfast as yours is!"

Their silence, or lack thereof, turned out to be irrelevant. What passed for Wes Edwards stepped out of the shadows at the far end of the hall, near the narrow door to the attic stair. He paid no attention to Kelleigh, but was instead glaring at Ben bringing up the rear with the last of the luggage.

"What is *he* doing here?" Wes's lip curled like that of a snarling dog. He turned his glare to Cally. "Callaghan, may I speak with you for a moment?"

Ben's expression, as he looked back at Wes, matched it for hostility. His right hand went to his left hip as if reaching for an invisible weapon. The young people in the hallway milled awkwardly. They thought they were witnessing ordinary human male rivalry, Cally realized, but she wondered if Ben could see through the stranger's glamour, could see who he really was.

She would have to ask him about it later. She needed to make sure the Fomorian stayed here at the Yellow House until nightfall so the queen and her warriors could deal with him. She couldn't have Ben driving him off just yet, and she certainly didn't want her son to watch Ben slay what Brandon believed to be his father with a legendary faerie sword.

Stepping between the two men with her palms outward, she said "It's alright." She looked at Ben until he took his eyes from the stranger and turned them to her. "I don't mind. I'll talk to him, just for a second. It'll be alright, I promise."

He didn't look like he quite shared her optimism, but Rosheen put a hand on his shoulder and whispered something into his ear. His hands dropped to his sides, though his shoulders remained rigid. "Alright," he said. "Just let me know if you need... anything."

"This way." Wes turned around and opened the narrow door behind him. Inside it, a steep stairway rose almost like a ladder. He turned around and ascended the steps two at a time, as if he had done it dozens of times before.

"What are you doing here?" Cally muttered as she climbed into the cobwebs and shadows behind him. She wasn't just asking about what he was doing here with her family; she also wondered why he felt so free to poke around in the attic of a home in which he was supposed to be a guest. "And what can you possibly have to say to me that hasn't already been said?"

Daylight filled the space beyond him. "I just want to show you something."

She mounted the last step and saw him standing with his back to her. He was looking out through the large, circular window which took up almost the entirety of the gable wall beneath the rafters. Cally felt for the amulet in her pocket, considering whether it might clear up for her, at last, exactly what this person was, but he turned around before she could act on her idea. His face bore what almost resembled a kindly smile in the midst of the skylit circle framing his head. He didn't speak, but gestured with one hand through the window. "Tell me what you see, out there."

Knowing better than to turn her back on him, she stepped behind him and looked over his shoulder. The window framed a picturesque, even for this time of year, view of the meadow on the other side of Gardens Road. Winter-yellow grass, shimmering in the breeze under the cloudy sky, softly clothed rolling hills all the way to the horizon. Usually, that was the only thing visible from here, but this time a massive tree broke the line of hills in the distance.

She had seen this tree before, though not always in just that spot. It's branches were not bare, as they should have been, but covered in a vibrant green. The longer Cally looked, the more they resembled verdant flames rising higher and higher into the sky.

"Do you see that?" he asked.

She didn't know whether or not to admit she could, or whether or not she should bring up the fact that the real Wes probably would not have been able to see it. When she didn't answer for several moments, he turned and looked at her over his shoulder. His smile had gone from kindly to gloating. "It's alright," he said in a low, saccharine voice. "I know you know I'm not really Wes Edwards."

It occurred to her that perhaps she should not have been so glib about assuring Ben she would be alright. She edged backwards toward the stairs.

"Callaghan McCarthy," he said, turning the rest of the way

around. "if I were going to harm you, I would have done it by now, and that pathetic excuse for a prince, waiting at the bottom of the stairs to rush to your aid, would still not have heard a thing. I thought you were smart enough to know things like that."

She stopped backing up, raising her chin in what she hoped was an expression of defiance. "Who are you, then?"

"I am an old friend of yours." His smirk became a leer.

"Your kind is not capable of understanding what friendship is."

He nodded, lowering his eyes for a second. "I must admit, you are right. But maybe you can teach me. There are many things for which I should thank you." Cally could only respond to this by furrowing her brow, so he elaborated. "I have been seeking that one," he said, nodding toward the stairs. "Wylldais's daughter. You call her Rosheen. My people have been seeking her for many years. Her mother disappeared, removing her to parts unknown the day she was conceived. Your sweetheart never even knew he'd sired her until she was gone beyond his reach. He still doesn't know who her mother is. He was a very libidinous young man in those days." He smirked, clearly expecting Cally to be wounded by this remark.

"I know all about his past," she said. "It's caused him more pain than it will ever cause me. Why have you been stalking Rosheen?"

"My dear, it's not Rosheen herself we're interested in. It's just the way all her bloodlines stack up, you see? She was a prime candidate to bring forth the Star back to Inverness, and now it is clear she is about to do so. *That* one, we must keep a very close eye on. We thought all hope was lost. We feared we would never find her or the young Star until it was too late. But now, in the greatest twist of fate, we have you to thank for bringing them right here to our doorstep."

Cally realized he was right, and that he meant for her to feel mortified about her unwitting complicity in this. Instead, she felt something feral rising within her, just beneath her solar plexus. She recognized the darker side of maternal instinct, the savage impulse to protect and defend.

"You have no right to interfere with this family." Her voice had become a low growl.

He waved a hand past his face in a gesture of unconcern. "In fact, I have every right," he replied levelly. "Rosheen's mother is a descendant of mine. Bloodlines are everything, to all fae folk. It's only a shame you have no clue about your own ancestry and how significant it is. You clearly never noticed, but we've also been tracking you for much of your life. You are why we recruited Eddie Teine, for instance, and..."

"You are not saying I also have faerie blood in me." She nearly spit the words out. "Don't even try."

"Oh, no, my dear, not a drop. Don't flatter yourself. Not a single drop! The blood that flows in your veins merely includes that of one of Faerie's oldest and most hated enemies. Even Rianwynn would despise you if she knew. Perhaps she does." He grinned and glanced out the window, licking his lips.

"I didn't come up here to argue genealogy with you," Cally said. "I just want you to leave my family alone. Just walk away. Pretend Wes Edwards got another boner for some young thing somewhere and went off in pursuit. His kids will buy that."

Her argument had a basic flaw: she was unable to follow it with a statement beginning with "or else I'll..."

He didn't point this out. "Everything's negotiable," he said with a shrug. Leaning back against the window frame, he put his hands into his pockets almost the way a real human would. "For instance, you might consider that you and I could form an alliance. I could go away, stay out of sight just as you wish, while together we quietly work together to mold young 'Adam' into the most powerful faerie king ever seen on this side of the ocean. On both sides, truly. There would be peace in Faerie at last, with the Sidhe finally subdued. You and I would be able to rule and guide this peaceful world together through him. Wouldn't you like that?"

She didn't bother telling him she would not. "Who *are* you?" she demanded, almost a little too loudly, hoping the people at the bottom of the stairs hadn't heard. She was almost certain now that this must, in fact, be Eladha. Her awareness of the glamour-busting amulet in her pocket made her thigh itch, but she knew if she drew it out to look at him now, he would only recognize it as yet another thing that rightfully belonged to him.

His human glamour didn't fade, but seemed to swell so that he loomed over her, a taller and much more powerful human than Wes Edwards had ever been. "You know who I am," he said. "And what I want to know is..."

"Dad?" Kelleigh's voice came up the stairway. "Dad, are you ever going to come down here and let me introduce Gordon to you, or do we have to come up there?"

Cally spun around when she heard footsteps starting up the stairs. "No, it's alright. We were just on our way down!"

21 – Not Just Any Wish

The kitchen of the Yellow House was far too small to accommodate the increased number of guests. While Faux-Wes helped Brandon, Kelleigh and Gordon uncover furniture in the seldom-used dining room, Cally took Rosheen and Ben aside into the living room. The three of them stood with their arms around one another, facing the tree as if discussing the decorations, while Cally explained what she had discovered.

"It's Eladha," she whispered in conclusion. "I'm ninety-nine percent sure of it." The silver cup, the gift supposedly from Wes to unborn Adam, had been nestled into the branches of the tree. She reached out with one finger to trace the fine engraving around its rim. The lettering spelled out the word "*Maponus.*" Cally didn't know what that meant, but she made a mental note to do an internet search on it as soon as possible.

"I think you're probably right," Ben was saying. "I couldn't see him, but I could feel him. I could feel the same...malice I felt when I fought him before. He would have killed me then, if it hadn't been for..."

"I'm sorry." Rosheen wasn't really looking at the tree. She seemed to be gazing right through it and through the wall to the meadow beyond. "I'm so sorry, for all of this. I should have stayed away. I should have stayed where I was."

Ben put his arms around his daughter and held her for a moment. "You have nothing to be sorry for," he assured her softly.

Cally agreed. "I'm just as glad as Brandon is that you're part of our family now."

Rosheen stood back and wiped her eyes, focusing on them at last. Her voice was still a little choked when she asked, "So Grandmother is coming here tonight?"

111

Cally had to grin at that. She knew Rianwynn Queen of Faerie hated to be called "Grandmother."

"According to Ana." Cally could hear footsteps in the hallway behind her, so she hurried to finish their conversation. "She says I'm to open the gate. I'm assuming that means she's planning to come through it and confront him. I doubt we're going to be able to continue keeping our secret, at that point."

"Well, Merry Solstice, I guess!" Rosheen let out a little, forced laugh that sounded, to Cally's ears, more like a sob. Reassembling her smile, she turned around as the others entered the room. "Unfortunately," she told them, "my father and your mother won't be able to stay for lunch after all. Father's noon shift at Auntie's store begins in a little while."

"Pity." The entity masquerading as Wes Edwards sat down on the couch as if he belonged there. Shooting a smirk at Ben he said, "But you'll be at the big Christmas party tomorrow night, right?"

"I..." Several expressions seemed to be wrestling for control of Ben's face, only mellowing when he looked at Rosheen. "I might be able to stop by the party for a few minutes before sunset," was all he could promise.

"Well I will *certainly* be there." Eladha served himself an eggnog as Brandon handed Cally's and Ben's jackets to them. "And, Callaghan, I'm looking forward to seeing you here for dinner tonight!"

Cally shut the door behind them without replying. "If all goes as I hope," she muttered, hurrying down the porch stairs, "he will *not* see me at dinner, and will definitely not be attending any Christmas parties, anywhere, ever!" She nearly broke into a sprint along the walkway to Gardens Road. "I just hope Rianwynn and her 'select warriors' don't storm the house like some kind of S.W.A.T. team when they show up to collect him."

"The queen is usually more subtle than that," Ben said as he hurried to keep up with her.

A cold wind was blowing sideways from the meadow by the time they reached the intersection with Main Street. From there, Cally could see into the Vale House front yard. Ignacio had finished stringing lights along the meadow fence and, though it was only early afternoon, someone had switched them on. A rainbow of festive colors swayed in the gray breeze, glowing warmly all the way from the street to the barn. Cally thought that would be a cheery sight for Ian and Sofie to return home to. She wondered if they were, in fact, already home.

She tugged her jacket shut against the chill and turned to look at Ben. "I guess you need to get back to work," she conceded. "Bree is going to read you the riot act as it is."

"It won't be the first time." He shook his head, smiling gently, but he was looking away, far down Main Street toward town. "Thank you for including me, today. It was nice to feel like a part of a real family, even if an old enemy happened to be there as well." He pulled her close to his side, putting himself – mostly – between her and the wind. "He's wrong, you know. I do remember Wylldais. I didn't know there was a baby until many years later, but I remember. I'm not a complete scoundrel."

"You were just a kid," Cally reassured. "They just used you to get what they wanted. But she... this Wylldais ...she must have been very beautiful. Rosheen certainly is."

"No, Rosheen gets that from me." He laughed, but then his face grew serious again. He nodded somberly toward the cracked length of curb in front of the news store. "So many different paths have led us to this place."

"A million little crossroads," she agreed. "When he was talking to me. Eladha, when he was telling me they've been watching me, too, it occurred to me... I mean, it would seem, ironically, that Wes actually saved me.

"The real Wes, I mean." She tried to speak above the wind without shouting loudly enough to broadcast her words to the whole neighborhood. "Back when I was young and stupid, when he talked me into getting married and leaving our hometown. If Eladha is telling the truth about his people having watched me all my life – and I don't see why he wouldn't be – then I escaped their eye for many years by letting Wes convince me to run off with him. I guess I should think more kindly of him. I could have ended up like Eddie Teine or..."

Feral gusts of wind kept trying to blow her hair into her face as she followed Ben's gaze. She could make out, just barely, the spot he was looking at. She'd fallen asleep in her car, just there, when she'd first arrived in Woodley.

"It was a sunny morning..." He turned his back to the scene, then, and faced her instead. Putting up a hand to stop her hair blowing across her face, he looked into her eyes. "I don't believe in destiny," he said. "Or the 'guiding hand of fate.' But that day I first saw you. There. Asleep in your car in front of the store, I knew. There was something about you. I knew I was going to fall in love with you."

"I was a mess," she reminded him. "All slumped against the seatbelt. It made a big crease across my face. I hope I wasn't drooling?"

"No, you weren't." He released her from his gaze and drew her close. "Or you were, I don't know. But I knew my life was about to change. And not just because you were the most beautiful woman I'd ever seen."

"Well, that's good, because I'm not."

He ignored this and went on. "What I could see. What I could tell, just looking at you then, was that you'd been through some stuff. Well, I guess we all have. But I saw something else. I think I understand now what it was: it was kindness. You were a person who hadn't let the blows of life make you hard. Instead, you always tried to make up for the harshness in the world by being kind to others. I saw a glimpse of that then, but I see it more and more clearly every day that I know you."

Cally tried to think of something cynical to say, to blunt the sting of tears in her eyes. She considered reminding him of all the times she would cheerfully have strangled someone for what had seemed to her to be good reasons at the time.

She decided to just kiss him instead. "After tonight," she reminded, "everything will be back to normal. Well, as normal as it ever gets around here." She stood back, holding her jacket shut against the wind once more. "But I do wish you could join us at the Christmas party tomorrow. I'd be dreading it a lot less if you...hey! Maybe I could make that my wish. Does this Real Santa have any authority to override Faerie law?" She gave him a mischievous grin to make sure he knew she was just teasing.

"In fact, he does." He did not return a mischievous grin, but he did smile as he reached behind himself. "So, kind lady, if you would do me this kindness." He pulled something out of his back pocket and handed it to her. She opened her palm to accept a length of paper, rolled up and tied in the middle with a thin, red ribbon. "Please put this into the basket on the mantel at Vale House for me, before the party tomorrow night, since I almost certainly will not be able to attend."

"Your wish." Her hand trembled as if the squashed roll of paper lying across it were some kind of sacred and powerful artifact.

"I hope you'll make a wish, too," he breathed. He didn't say, *"I hope you'll make the same wish I'm making,"* but she knew what he meant without his having to say it.

22 – Tacos for Santa

As Cally passed between the gateposts, she craned her neck to look down the slope of the lawn toward the pond. Where a few hours ago there had been only an ice-bound pier, now a large, old fishing boat listed against the bank.

She broke into a run up the flagstone walk, flinging herself across the porch and through the door. "Ian and Sofie are back!" she called, but the Hall was empty. Apparently everyone else already knew the Vale House proprietors had returned. They were all sitting around the dining room table, talking cheerfully and passing the brandy decanter. Katarina turned in her seat and waved over her shoulder through the doorway.

"Cally! There you are! Come on and join us!"

At the head of the table sat a handsome, white-haired gentleman with a much deeper tan than he'd had the last time Cally had seen him. He was smiling and joking just as he always had, as if he'd never been away. A waiflike white-haired woman sat quietly at his left hand, gazing into her brandy glass and slowly turning the stem between her fingers in much the same way Nell often did. Nell herself was not toying with her glass but was smiling hugely at her parents.

The seat at Ian's right hand was set with an empty brandy glass waiting for Cally. Ignacio reached to fill it, but Cally dashed right past it to Ian. He struggled to stand up (probably to assist her with her seat as a proper Southern gentleman would) but she had wrapped her arms around his shoulders before he could quite get his chair pushed back.

"Oh, it's so good to see you!" She absolutely meant it. "I finally feel like it really is Christmas, now!"

Standing back to beam at him, she thought he looked more

like Santa Claus than any of her previous suspects. In that moment she was so pleased to see him, sitting at the head of the dining table where he belonged, she really was ready to believe hc was Santa, or at least that Santa had granted her wish to see him there again at last.

She regarded Sofie, as well, the perfect image of Mrs. Claus, if a bit thin, and tried to catch her eye. Sofie was smiling but not meeting anyone's gaze, and Cally wondered if she would be open to being hugged. The presence of too many people often made Sofie anxious.

She went around the back of Ian's chair to Sofie's side of the table. She thought Sofie might be intimidated by someone bending over her, so she knelt on one knee beside the old woman and offered her hand. "Mrs. May, it's so nice to see you," she said. "I hope you had a pleasant journey?"

Sofie did meet her eyes, fleetingly, and her smile was wide, but she looked away quickly and did not reach back to Cally's hand. "There were so many faeries!" she said to the china cabinet behind Ian. "But I missed our ghosts!"

Everyone smiled indulgently. Sofie often said things like this, but nobody at Vale House judged her. Least of all people like Nell and Cally who knew that, despite Sofie's illness, she really wasn't hallucinating when she spoke of faeries and ghosts, at least, not most of the time. Cally ventured a gentle pat on the old woman's knee before rising and returning to her seat, which Ignacio had hurried to pull out from the table for her so Ian would stop trying to stand up.

"Ian was telling us all about his adventure!" Bethany said as Cally sat down. "I'm sorry you missed so much of the story. But I'm sure you have a story or two you can tell us now, yourself?" She inclined her head toward the south end of the house, the direction in which the Yellow House lay.

"All I can say right now is..." Cally began, but was interrupted by the sound of Katarina loudly clearing her throat. "...that I'm sure Ian's story is much more suitable for listening to at the table," she concluded.

"You didn't miss much, Ms. McCarthy," Ian said. "I had just begun to tell how we passed by Bald Head Island on the Intracoastal

117

Waterway and..."

Cally picked up the glass of brandy Ignacio pushed toward her and listened to Ian continue his tale. She wondered if she had missed the part about how he had managed to get his run-down trawler to an ocean that lay over two hundred miles to the east, or if he had simply not offered any explanation. She suspected the latter. She didn't care. It was simply delightful to have the master of Vale House sitting in his proper place at the head of the table, telling stories as he always did. Sofie smiled and nodded at everything he said, sometimes applauding when he described certain landmarks, even when the names of them started to sound less and less like any place Cally had ever heard of before.

"But I am monopolizing the conversation," he said after concluding a description of a place called "Talonbrook" which, apparently, had lovely weather all year round. "I would like to raise my glass to Ms. McCarthy, here, and thank her for stepping into my shoes and managing this Bed and Breakfast in my absence." He started to raise said glass, but noticed it was empty. Ignacio rushed to top up all of the glasses around the table.

"Ian, I don't think anyone could ever fill your shoes," Cally said. "Honestly, all I do is paperwork. Kat and Ignacio and Bethany do all the actual work."

Ian raised his refilled glass anyway, and gave her a wink over the top of it as he drank to her. Cally saluted him with her own glass. She knew he wasn't really talking about managing the paperwork, but about acting as the diplomatic liaison between Woodley and its faerie Neighbors on the other side of the meadow fence. Ian had appointed her as his replacement in this capacity before he'd gone off sailing, but she felt like she was the one who was completely at sea. She wished there were some way he could teach her more about the job before he went away again or before he, ultimately, went away forever.

"Maybe that should be my wish," she murmured into her glass.

Everyone looked up from their own drinks.

"What should?" Bethany asked. "No, don't tell us. If you do, it won't come true!"

"Sorry." She grinned sheepishly. "I didn't realize I'd said that out loud. What else did I say?"

"I shouldn't tell you! You keep going on about young Ben!" Katarina drained her glass and stood up. "And now you must all excuse me. I have more tortillas to make – I only have eight dozen so far."

"Kat!" Cally was the only person who seemed to think this was excessive. "Eight dozen?"

"People like my tacos!" Katarina shrugged. "I only need to make about two dozen more. Three, to be safe. Santa eats more than most people, you know!" She turned, laughing, toward the back hall.

23 – Message from No One

Cally felt a little bad about Katarina working all alone in the kitchen, so she left the table while everyone else was still chatting merrily about the upcoming festivities. She paused long enough to whisper, not altogether untruthfully, into Bethany's ear that she had not heard anything new from the sheriff, then she followed Doctor Boojums down the back hall to the kitchen.

"Kat, you don't use a tortilla press?" she asked when she entered to find the cook patting dough between her hands.

"Don't be silly!" The flour-dusted Christmas tree on the front of Katarina's apron looked like it was covered in snow. "You have to use your hands! It's the only way to put your love into them!"

"Can I help?" Not waiting for an answer, she picked up one of the balls of dough and squeezed it between her palms. "I just hate the thought of you still hard at work while everyone else has, apparently, already started the party."

Katarina laughed. "Well, *someone* needs to stay sober enough to serve dinner tonight. Dinner, by the way, will be pizza delivered by Luke. Would you like some sangria?" Katarina nodded toward the half empty pitcher on the work table, then turned to lay her finished tortilla onto the griddle covering four of the stove burners.

Cally shook her head, smiling. "Thanks, but I need to stay sober, too, for...something I need to accomplish tonight." She looked at the flattened dough in her hands and swore. "I don't think I'm as good at this as you are, Kat. This thing is shaped like the state of Maryland."

Katarina turned around to look at it. "It's perfect!" she said, taking it from Cally's hands and slapping it down onto the griddle without trying to make it even the slightest bit rounder. "You don't want to overwork the dough!"

Cally tried again to make a perfectly round, perfectly flat tortilla like the ones that seemed to emerge magically from between Katarina's hands. She managed to make one shaped like Illinois and one shaped like Texas (her best so far, she thought) while Katarina produced at least a dozen more, shaped like tortillas. She finally gave up and said, "Okay, maybe I can find some other way to make myself useful until... Thanks for being patient with me."

She used the backstairs to sneak up to her room so she wouldn't have to pass through the dining room and make excuses for not sitting back down. It occurred to her, as she reached the upstairs hallway, that she hadn't seen George in a while. Walking swiftly past the gallery (where she could still hear the cheerful voices of the household rising from the dining room) she peered down the main stairway into the Hall. The Preacher's morose ghost brooded in front of the desk, but George was not there.

"Well," she thought. "While he's not looking..." She crept back to the north end of the hallway and opened the drawer of the butler's desk. Reaching all the way to the back, she dug into the mess of bent paperclips and wrinkled envelopes until her fingers found a triangular piece of wood. "Gotcha!" She straightened, tucking it into her waistband, and covered it with her blouse before turning around. To her relief, she still saw no sign of George. She shut the drawer and ran down the stairs, ignoring the Preacher as she passed behind him.

Once inside the parlor, she took the *zemi* from beneath her clothing and regarded it. Each edge of the triangle had been deeply and cleverly carved to resemble a face. Each face bore a different expression, though only one of them looked human. The talisman also bore a few chew-marks from a short adventure it had once had with a dog, but otherwise it was very well preserved.

Cally grinned at it and imagined the conversation she would have with George on Christmas Eve. *"Why don't you go into the parlor and talk to Santa?"* she would suggest, and he would say, *"Cally, you know I can't do that. It's too far away from my* zemi.*"* and then she would say, *"Oh, no, it's not. I put your* zemi *in there*

121

already!" and he would say *"But how can that be? We're all the way up here by the butler's desk..."* and then he would suddenly understand. It was perfect! She chuckled to herself and placed the wooden carving into the red basket on the mantle, carefully burying it beneath all the paper wishing-scrolls already there.

Then she took from her pocket the little scroll Ben had given her. Doing her best to un-flatten it and plump up the ribbon bow, she nestled it in amongst the other wishes.

"There you are, my love," she murmured. "For what it's worth. I hope it comes true."

Stepping back, she regarded the full basket. Of course, even if wishes did come true, Ben's could not unless she wished the same thing. She had no doubt his wish was to find a way to make the impossible possible, for the two of them to be together at last like an ordinary couple. Perhaps there really was a Santa Claus who could trump Rianwynn's Faerie Queen card and free Ben of his obligations to her kingdom. Probably not, but even if there were, unless she made it clear this was her wish as well, his wish would be invalid according to the rule about not making wishes that interfered with others' free will.

Well, it was certainly something she wanted. What could it hurt to say so?

Bethany had left a stack of Vale House stationery next to the basket on the mantel, and a candy-dish filled with lengths of different colored ribbons. She took one of the sheets and a piece of purple ribbon and went back to her office.

Setting the paper down on the desk blotter, she reached into a drawer to find one of the exquisite pens people had been giving her every birthday and Christmas since she'd officially "become a writer." She had never used any of them, because until now she'd never felt she had anything special enough to write with them. The lacquered green one would be perfect, she thought, and tested it on the back of a utility bill. It made only scratch-marks – the ink would not flow. She said a mild curse-word, but the metaphor about things that dry up and become useless over time if never used went completely over her head. She found herself staring at the message indicator blinking through her screen-saver.

"Alright," she said. "A little advice from a friend would be good right now." Especially from a friend who had always encouraged her to take leaps of faith which had always, so far, made her life better. She smiled and wiggled her computer mouse to clear the screen-saver.

Instead of the chat program, though, a large dialog box sat in the center of the screen. It looked like an error message, with the usual "OK" and "Cancel" buttons at the bottom, but the message itself was only one word.

Help

Muttering a mild curse word, she stared at it a moment, and then clicked the "OK" button. The dialog box disappeared, only to be replaced by a new one reading: *I need your help.*

She said a much less mild curse-word and quickly opened the chat program.

Cally>> Em are you okay? What's the matter?

Emerald didn't reply right away. There was nothing unusual about that, but this time Cally couldn't bear to just sit there staring into the screen, waiting. She got up and paced around the desk to keep herself calm. She looked out the office window as she paced past it and noticed it was starting to get dark outside. She sat down again, ready to send a slightly more panicky query, but a reply from Emerald appeared at last.

> **Emerald<<** I'm fine Cally - - I only wanted to know if you heard any more news about that body
>
> **Cally>>** Oh thank god. I was worried that message was from you.
>
> **Emerald<<** What message?
>
> **Cally>>** It just says "help."

Emerald<< Who is it from?

Cally>> I don't know. It doesn't say. It's just a plain dialog box.

Cally>> Oh shit. I bet it's a virus. And I just clicked OK on it!

Emerald<< LOL silly! Never try to open a mysterious message from nobody!

Cally>> Yeah, I wasn't thinking.

Cally>> Damn it. Taking my computer over to Luke for repairs was not on my list of things I need to do tonight.

She glanced up again at the window. It was definitely dark outside, now. She was glad Emerald was alright, and she didn't want to be late again.

Cally>> Listen Em, I gotta run. Ben is probably already here.

Cally>> I'll talk to you later.

Cally>> Hopefully not TOO much later.

24 – Cally Opens the Gate

Ben stood with his back to the Christmas lights along the fence. They swung in the fitful wind as she ran, still pulling on her jacket, across the lawn to him.

"She's here," Ben said when she reached up to wrap her arms around him.

"Who is? Oh. The queen." She let her arms drop to her sides. "I thought we were at least going to have our few minutes together." Then she raised her chin and lifted her arms again, slipping them around him and kissing him firmly.

He returned her embrace and her kiss, but she could feel his lips curling as he tried not to smile. Finally he did have to push her back and give her a laughing look. "I thought your job as Armadeur was to prevent war with Faerie, not incite it?"

She tried to find words to tell him she had never loved him more than she did in that moment. She settled for, "Alright, then, let's not keep her majesty waiting."

Taking him by the hand, she led the way along the fence to where it met the masonry pillars at the edge of the Vale House grounds. On the other side of them, the old metal gate which marked the end of Main Street sagged across the entrance to the meadow. Cally could see only shadows wavering in the darkness beyond it. She peered carefully into them as Ben followed her to the gate. For a moment, the moon peeked through the cloud cover and brushed a streak of silver through a swath of armor-clad chests, chins, and shoulders.

Cally lifted the loop of chain, which served as the only "lock" on the gate, over the fencepost. Ben bent and linked his hands under the gate's middle rail. A sharp, female voice spoke from the shadows on the other side.

"No. *She* has to do it."

Ben smiled sideways at Cally. "Of course," he called into the darkness. "I'm only going to help her."

Cally bent beside him and together they dragged the gate across the ground, inscribing a semi-circle of disrupted turf into the meadow. When she straightened, she found herself looking into the eyes of at least two dozen icily beautiful faerie women, each clad in gleaming armor of silver and adamant. They would have looked like a regiment of statues, Cally thought, but for their hair of myriad colors flying in the wind. One tall, pale figure stood beside them, and a host of shadows loomed behind them.

The lone woman stepped forward without making a sound through the dry, windswept grass. Though she bore a naked sword which matched the pale gold of her hair, she was clad only in flowing silk, far too thin, Cally thought, for the weather. A golden circlet, adorned with green gems glowing like fireflies in the moonlight, bound her brow.

"Rianwynn Queen of Faerie." Cally bowed deeply. "Hail and well met."

The woman regarded her stonily. "Very pretty words for a mortal."

It occurred to Cally that Bree might well have got her warmth and charm from her mother. She kept this thought to herself and turned, gesturing with one hand toward the porch lights along Gardens Road. "He's in the third house. There. The other people in the house are my family...our family," she corrected, mustering the nerve to look Rianwynn directly in her cool, gray eyes. "I would appreciate it if you could extract him without upsetting the rest of them."

"What is he doing in there?" was Rianwynn's reply.

"What? I don't know. Probably sitting down to dinner. It doesn't matter..."

"You were supposed to bring him out here. To the gate, where we could apprehend him without causing an incident."

"Nobody told me that!" Cally's scowl swept the regimented Sidhe warriors. None of them appeared to be Ana. But then, Ana would never wear a uniform or stand quietly in rank. Perhaps she was one of the dark, shadowy forms lurking in the background.

"We can't very well go storming into a human household," Rianwynn said. "There would be repercussions for such an action!"

Cally had to admit that made sense. "How am I going to get him to come out here, though?" She regretted saying this aloud as soon as the words were out of her mouth. The look Rianwynn gave her would have withered an oak tree.

"At least let us walk with her as far as the house," came a voice from among the queen's assembled soldiers. Cally thought she recognized the voice, and when she looked she saw one of the Sidhe women separate herself from the fore of the ranks. "In case she needs protection." The woman met Cally's eye and smiled, nodding imperceptibly. It was the closest thing Cally had ever experienced to having a faerie bow to her.

She recognized Aileen, Rianwynn's lieutenant and also, as it happened, Ana's mother. Aileen had never seemed to hold any ill will toward Cally over her relationship with Ben, and had in the past almost seemed to behave as a friend. Cally bowed back to her, a real bow, though not a deep one.

The queen acceded to Aileen's suggestion, but when Ben moved to follow Cally back out through the gate, she barked "You will remain here!" Before he could open his mouth to protest, she nodded to her ranked warriors and four of them stepped aside to surround him. In a voice like distant thunder, Rianwynn intoned, "It is now your time to be in *my* world." She waved a hand across the dark sky. "As you are well aware, you may not return to the human side of this fence until daybreak."

None of the Sidhe appeared to be physically restraining Ben, but the way he stood in the grass, stony-faced with his arms bent at his sides, gave Cally the impression he was straining mightily against his impulse to disobey.

The rest of the armed Sidhe followed their queen through the gate and assembled around Cally. She hated to leave Ben standing there watching her, but she steeled herself to turn away and lead the queen and her soldiers along Gardens Road. The sooner this thing was over and done with, the sooner Eladha was gone, the better.

"Be silent; do not show yourselves," was the last thing Cally heard Rianwynn say before she slipped into the shadows of the fence along the road. At her word, the warriors also seemed to dissolve into the grass at the verge. Cally thought maybe they had taken on new glamours and disguised themselves as fenceposts – she didn't really know how these things worked. Only one of them remained visible to her: Aileen strode at Cally's side on long, perfect warrior legs, a gem-studded scabbard swinging from her hip, ruby hair flying behind her like a cloak in the wind. When they drew abreast of the Yellow House, she laid a hand on Cally's arm and stopped.

"Get him to come outside," she said. "We will act as soon as he steps down off the parapet."

"Parapet? Do you mean porch?"

"If that's what you call it." Aileen nodded into the glow of the antique plastic snowman illuminating the front door, then turned to Cally, silently drawing her sword. "Good luck," she said as she dissolved backwards into the shadows.

25 – A Final Confrontversation

She ascended the stair slowly, pausing on each step as if the next one loomed yards above her head. When she reached for the front door handle she could hear Kelleigh's voice inside, calling a question to someone, and she could smell another of Brandon's culinary concoctions cooking. She wished she really were just arriving for a quiet little holiday get-together with her family. Even sitting at a meal with the real Wes Edwards would have been better than what was about to happen.

No sign of movement could be seen in the kitchen at the far end of the entryway, but she could see light coming from the dining room doorway. She leaned to the right of the door to peer into the dining room window. Through green lace curtains she could see the table laden with antique serving dishes. Rosheen sat at the far end; Kelleigh's back was to her. Wes (only not Wes) sat on the opposite side of the table, facing her, laughing at something Gordon (out of sight at the other end of the room) had said.

It was a charming illusion, and Cally was greatly tempted to succumb to it. Instead, she slipped the crescent-moon amulet out of her pocket and raised it to her eye. Squinting through the crystal felt to her like looking through a sophisticated camera lens, instantly bringing myriad unnoticed details into focus. Wes's visage became a blur, dissolving until the scaly, red skin of the Fomorian general could be seen beneath it. Its jaw full of daggerlike teeth laughed at Brandon's jokes; its yellow-slit eyes followed Rosheen's every move.

Cally lowered the crystal and looked again at the commonplace family dinner scene. But now, no matter how enthusiastically Faux-Wes laughed, how gallantly he raised his glass in a toast, Cally could no longer un-see the too-wide toothiness of his jaw or the reptilian gleam in his eye. She put the amulet back in her pocket. "No," she muttered at him. "You cannot stay here. Once the baby arrives, you will dispose of the others just like you did with Eddie Teine. Just like you did with the real Wes."

As if he had heard her, his eyes flicked up to meet hers through the curtain. His too-wide smile grew even wider. "Ah!" he said as Brandon leaned into view with a freshly-opened wine bottle. "Your mother is here! Don't get up. I'll let her in!"

He appeared in the door much more quickly than he should have been able to. Cally nearly jumped out of her skin as he flung it open crying, "Callaghan! How lovely to see you!"

Well, she thought, at least he was closer, now, to where she needed him to be. She did her best to return his friendly smile. "Can I talk to you for a minute? Wes?"

"Of course!" He stepped back, holding the door wider.

"In private. Please." She stepped backward, herself, to make room for him.

He turned and called over his shoulder into the house. "I'll just be a moment!" As calls of acknowledgement came from within, he came out onto the porch and shut the door behind him.

Cally wished the Sidhe warriors would just come up onto the porch and apprehend him without further ado, but no order to charge came from the shadows along the fence behind her, no faerie warriors swarmed over the porch railings. She wondered how she was going to get him to step off the porch as Aileen had instructed.

"I'm so glad you've decided to join us after all," he was saying. "It will feel so right and good to have you sitting at the table with us, just like a real family again."

"Cut the crap," she snapped before she could think of something more politic to say. "We were never a real family."

His look of feigned hurt was almost convincing. "Calla... Cally. Don't you believe you and I can work together? I promise I can make it worth your while." His friendly smile widened into what was almost a leer.

"I'm sure you can," she said. "Just like you did for Eddie Teine."

A spark flared in his eyes for the briefest moment, but his

smile quickly reassembled itself. "Mr. Teine's demise was his own doing," he explained in patient tones. "He resigned his contract of his own free will, resulting in cessation of the benefits for which he had signed up. His blood is not on the hands of any of my people."

"And what about the real Wes?" She took a step back, closer to the porch steps. "Eladha, I thought you were the one who always tried to make humans out to be faerie-killers, not the other way around."

His teeth flashed in a snarl when she called him by his real name. She stepped backwards again, not fully pretending to be intimidated by this, and succeeded in drawing him one step closer to the stairs.

He made no further attempt to hide the malice in his eyes. To Cally it seemed that his human face became almost translucent; she could swear she saw the ruddy visage of the Formorian even without the crystal talisman.

"The truce is broken," he reminded her. "A human broke it. Now I can do whatever I want. Even so, I did not kill your precious ex." He smiled what she supposed was meant to be reassurance.

"Then how do you explain the body I saw?" She took one more step backwards and put her hand on the column at the top of the stair railing.

Past his shoulder, she saw movement through the little arched window in the door. She glanced to see Rosheen peering out at her with wide, concerned eyes. Eladha, apparently noting her glance, tilted his head toward the door. "I'm not planning any harm to them," he said, "If that's what you're worried about. We really are all family, now. Isn't that a beautiful thing, to you humans? Come." He reached a too-long, too-pale hand out to her, and if she hadn't been holding onto the porch column she would have stepped back again and fallen down the steps.

"Come," he repeated, his voice no longer Wes's but still a very good imitation of gentleness. "Be a part of our special family. I am only here to ensure young Adam grows up right. I know you want the same for him. You can play the part of the wayward wife reunited at last with her longsuffering husband. It will be a happy story for your children to tell one another. And someday, when the

Star comes of age, you will rule at my side. I can reward you very richly for your allegiance." His tender smile morphed into a blatant leer, then, and he laid a cool hand on her shoulder. Though she managed to control her instinct to shrink like terrified prey, her skin felt like it was trying to crawl right off her body.

Swallowing, she inclined her head toward the steps. "Let's take a walk," she said, "so we can talk more privately." She dared a glance into the shadows on the far side of the road, but the grass along the fence appeared utterly devoid of any crouching shadows or faerie warriors. Taking a long, slow breath, she turned her back to Eladha and stepped down one stair.

As she did, his hand slid from her shoulder to the back of her neck. She clenched her teeth to hold back a scream as she felt the prick of a single claw against her skin. If he chose, she knew, he could drive that claw straight into her spine.

And still, no shadows erupted from along the fence to rush to her aid.

He stepped softly down to stand on the step beside her. "No," he whispered into her ear. "You come back inside. Stay with us; stay with me! Forget that other one, Rianwynn's son. He is weak. He will not fight for you. He has already told you numerous times: he would just let you walk away. But I would never do that. Come and let me teach you bliss few mortal women will ever know."

She couldn't help jerking away from him, then, throwing her arm up over her head to knock his hand away. His claw dragged like a razor around the back of her neck as she spun to face him.

There was no mistaking his face for that of any human, now. Eladha, General of the Fomorians, ran his serpent-like tongue across the tips of his teeth and hissed, "You would be a goddess! What is the matter with you people? You *humans!*"

He seemed to expect her to react to this as if it had been an egregious insult, but she smiled. "Yes. We humans." She reached down to grasp the rusty Christmas tree stand beside her leg. He lurched forward to take it from her but stopped, when he realized what it was, jerking his hands back and holding them up before her.

"Don't..." was all he had time to say before Cally put her weight behind the rusty iron and shoved it into his chest.

Letting out an ultrasonic screech, he flailed at the object as if it were a mass of striking vipers. She only just managed to jump out of the way as he curled into a fetal ball around it and tumbled down the stairs.

The Sidhe emerged from the shadows beyond the road, then, like ghosts stepping through a wall. They quickly surrounded Eladha's writhing form, but they did not go near him. Even the queen stared in horror as he shrieked soundlessly and rolled upon the lawn, clawing at his chest. The iron seemed to cling to his flesh as if electrified. When he grasped at it, his hands fused to it.

"Get if off him!" Rianwynn ordered.

Cally wondered why the queen would show such compassion toward her old enemy, but then she understood: none of them could do anything as long as he was in contact with iron. She reached out to the rusted reindeer-leg projecting from between Eladha's arms, bracing herself as if his agony would be transmitted to her when she touched it.

It was nothing, to her touch, but cold metal. She pulled the iron object away and flung it into the road, genuinely surprised not to see large chunks of Eladha's flesh flying away still attached to it. When she turned back to look, he appeared to be unscathed, though unmoving.

The Sidhe warriors took no chances on him recovering his strength. They fenced him in with swords and with lances, and Aileen drew him to his feet by his hair. Other soldiers pulled his arms behind his back and bound them with what looked, to Cally, like a living length of silver silk.

"You will not get away from us so easily again," Rianwynn declared. Standing before the queen, subdued, he looked up at the sky with what almost seemed like an expression of relief on his face, as if he were glad to be back among fey kind again at last.

While the queen and her soldiers marched their captive away at the points of their faerie blades, Aileen remained behind. She reached through Cally's hair to touch the back of her neck, and drew away pale fingers tipped with bright blood.

"It's just a scratch," Cally insisted.

Aileen shook her head and began unlacing the pouch at her

belt. "There might be toxins. Come let me tend to you."

"I should go back inside, before someone comes out to look for me. I need to tell them... My god, what will I tell them?"

"Rosheen was watching the whole time," Aileen reminded her, slipping an arm around her and urging her toward the road. "She'll think of something. Much cleverer than her sister, that one."

They walked back to the gate, arriving in time to see the silver shadows, still trailed by a host of darker ones, disappearing across the meadow. Cally knew Ben was among them – she hadn't been able to say goodbye to him. While Aileen rubbed a salve on the back of her neck that smelled, somehow, like she imagined diamonds would smell if diamonds had a smell, she muttered, "He must think I'm the worst excuse for a soul-mate that ever existed."

"He doesn't," said Aileen. "He thinks every second he gets to spend with you is more riches than he will ever deserve." She replaced the salve into her belt. "But he does wish you would make a wish."

"You talk to him about things like that?" Cally didn't even remember to be annoyed at the topic of wishes being brought up again. "He confides this sort of thing to you?"

"I am his friend," Aileen replied simply, standing back and re-distributing Cally's hair around her shoulders. "Were you thinking you and I should fight over him? I would kick your ass, you know." Her laughter rang out over the hills. "There would be nothing left for him to love!"

Cally looked at the flawlessly beautiful Sidhe warrior. "Maybe you really are, what Rianwynn would call, a more suitable mate for him."

Aileen snorted. "I am! But he wants love. We Sidhe can be very good friends. Our friendship is powerful and deathless. But we aren't much good at love." She waved a hand in the direction Ben had gone. "*He* has too much human in him – he is absolutely besotted with you."

Cally had to smile, then. "Lieutenant, if you ever do kick my ass, I will consider it an honor."

"Close the gate behind me." Aileen said as she stepped into the meadow. "And don't forget to make a wish."

Cally let out a sigh. "Wishing breaks your heart," she murmured for the hundredth time, not really to Aileen, who was already walking away. "The other shoe always drops."

But that, just before the faerie woman passed out of sight, reminded Cally of what Michael had told her, that the next time she was in the presence of faeries she should look at their feet. She drew the moon-shaped amulet from her pocket once more, raising it quickly to her eye to catch the last glimpse of the warrior's silver boots as she departed.

Except she wasn't wearing boots. Through the crystal, Cally could see that the faerie woman wasn't wearing any shoes at all.

She shut the gate and went back to the Yellow House.

"I told everyone," Rosheen said solemnly as Cally entered the dining room, "about the argument you and Wes had. I guess it was a pretty bad one? He stormed off down the street."

Cally smiled her thanks to the young woman. "I'm so sorry about all of this," she said to the others seated around the table.

"It's not your fault, Mom." Kelleigh patted the tablecloth next to her, encouraging Cally to sit down. "That's just the way he is."

"He always pulls stuff like this," Brandon reminded her. "But he always comes waltzing back like nothing ever happened."

"Who knows," said Kelleigh. "He might be back in time for dessert!" Her laughter was convincing, but her face didn't match it.

Cally didn't know what else to do. She sat down and accepted the platter Gordon passed to her. It held what looked like a beautifully garnished roast of pork or beef, but on closer examination turned out to actually be made of wild rice and mushrooms.

"Gravy?" Brandon offered.

"Oh, look!" Rosheen jumped up from her seat and ran to the window. "Look, it's starting to snow!"

December

24

Christmas Eve

20 –   Frittata's Taco

In the gray light of dawn, Ben slipped under the covers next to Cally. "I've come to deliver one of your Christmas presents a little early."

She stretched herself along his warm length and murmured, "I can't wait to open it." Past his shoulder, she could see snow still drifting gently down outside the casement windows.

"I always enjoy our mornings together." He propped himself up on one elbow and smiled down at her. "But that's not what I was talking about. I'm referring to a gift the queen has sent to you, by way of me."

Reaching up, she traced the crinkles that ran from the corner of his eye to his temple. "I can't think of any better gift than you being here with me."

"Well, that's just it." His eye-crinkles deepened when his smile widened. "She says, in return for the help you gave last night, she has invoked a special dispensation to allow me to stay for the Christmas party tonight."

"That's wonderful!" She propped herself up on her own elbow, then. "It'll be so nice to have you here!"

"There's just one catch."

"Ugh." She sank back down onto her pillow, thinking several crude words. Aloud, she said "Of course there is."

"It's not a terrible catch. It's just that I have to leave at midnight."

"Or what? You'll turn into a pumpkin?"

"Something like that. Who knows?"

"Well, it's still a wonderful present." She pulled him down onto the pillow beside her and did her best to forget that she had still not prepared the wish she was supposed to have ready for the party

139

under discussion. She could worry about that later.

Neither Bethany nor George were sitting behind the tinsel tree on the reception desk when they went downstairs. "Bethany is taking the rest of the year off," Cally told Ben, but then she heard humming in the parlor. She put her head through the parlor doorway. "You're supposed to be taking the rest of the year off!"

"Well I'm not staying home alone on Christmas Eve!" Bethany was standing beside what was meant to resemble a beautiful, old fashioned arch-front radio but was actually a modern stereo on the inside. A stack of CDs teetered on the Queen Anne table beside it. "I've got to pick out the music for tonight. Do you like Bing Crosby?"

"Come have breakfast with us," Ben encouraged futilely.

"Just bring me a refill when you're done." Bethany handed him her empty mug and opened a CD case. Cally didn't argue. At least Bethany wasn't asking if she'd heard anything new from the sheriff.

When they arrived in the kitchen, Katarina was at the stove busily stirring a massive pot. Ben inhaled deeply and said, as he always did, "Kat, that smells delicious!"

Katarina laughed. "It does, but it's not breakfast! This is the taco filling – it has to cook all day!" She waved her wooden spoon toward the counter beside the coffee maker. "Today we'll have to make do with fresh pastries from the Bean Garden." She turned back to her simmering pot.

Cally understood at last what a strong man Ben truly was when he did not allow his disappointment to show. He smiled gently and crossed the room to peer into the pink paper box from Andi Kilmarten's coffee shop. Inside was an assortment of pastries and muffins, some decorated with red and green sprinkles.

"They do look festive," Cally acknowledged as Ben began filling coffee mugs. She offered to microwave a danish for him. Behind her, Katarina sighed and put down her spoon.

"Hold on a second. Wait!" The cook had turned around and

was looking at Ben with big, sympathetic eyes. "Here, hand me a plate."

While Ben got a plate out of the cupboard, Katarina spooned some of the taco filling into a skillet. When the mixture – in which the chilis were still quite green and crisp – began to sizzle, she cracked two eggs into a bowl and whisked them together. These she poured over the meat and peppers in the pan and waited, spatula poised.

"There you are!" she announced triumphantly, sliding the improvised hot meal onto the plate. *"Frittatas taco!"* Ben thanked her warmly and sat down at the work table. Katarina watched him, beaming, spatula held aloft like a scepter. "Cally, you want some too?" she asked as an afterthought.

"Thank you, Kat. It's really sweet of you, but I'm quite content with my danish." She looked out through the back door. The back yard glistened like a white sugar wonderland. The snow, piling up to a point on the gazebo roof, made it resemble an upside-down ice-cream cone. Two lines of footprints ran from the back door to the little stone cottage at the rear of the garden. No footprints ran, as far as she could tell, from the side gate. She started to ask Katarina if she'd seen the sheriff yet this morning, but stopped herself in time.

Instead she said "By the way, Kat. It looks like Ben's going to be able to join us for the party tonight."

"Well, it's about time, young Bennet!" Katarina turned back to stirring her pot. "We've only invited you every single year since, well, since I've been here, and that's a long time! You should convince your sister to come, too!"

Ben promised he'd try. Cally refilled Bethany's coffee mug and took it with her when she and Ben walked to the front door. To the tune of a Bob Hope song drifting in from the parlor, she let the coffee grow cool on the reception desk while she gave Ben a long and proper goodbye kiss.

The big, brass sleigh bell Ignacio had hung on the doorknob jangled when she opened it to see him off, late again for work. "I'll see you this evening," he promised as he stepped outside into the snow.

27 – A Game of Soldiers

Bethany, singing along to "*It's Beginning To Look A Lot Like Christmas*," paused to take a deep slurp of the cooled coffee, but made no complaint as she continued singing and sorting CDs. Ignacio was in the parlor now, as well, stacking white birch logs in preparation for the annual lighting of the parlor side of the hearth. "Do you have any Trans-Siberian Orchestra?" he asked Bethany.

"I can lend you my old MP3 player," Cally offered. "It has hundreds of songs, and you won't have to go back and forth changing discs all evening."

Bethany gave her a deer-in-the headlights look. "I don't think I should try anything newfangled, this close to the party. People will start arriving in just a few hours! Anyway I don't even know if it would work with this stereo..."

Ignacio, however, assured them both he could make it work. "I really do like the Trans-Siberian Orchestra," he said, so Cally hurried up the stairs to find her old MP3 player. She'd placed it in the butler's desk, along with an outdated eBook reader, so that George could read and listen any time he wanted.

She still didn't see him anywhere, as she opened the old desk at the end of the upstairs hallway, but in case he was listening she said aloud, "I'm just going to borrow my music player for tonight. I promise I'll put it back."

Hurrying back down the stairs, she delivered the device into Bethany's skeptical hands.

"I don't know..." Bethany squinted at the end of the dangling cable.

Before Cally could show her the USB port in the back of the stereo, a phone began ringing on the far side of the Hall.

"Ugh, my office line," Cally said.

"Don't worry, I've got this." Ignacio winked at Cally and took the player from Bethany.

Cally apologized over her shoulder as she ran back across the Hall. "It's probably Kelleigh or..." She thought she knew (and knew she wasn't going to like) what her children must be calling to ask, but when she yanked the office door open and snatched up the receiver, it was Sheriff Mahon's voice on the other end of the line.

"Sorry," he said. "I tried to call the main house line, but it's been forwarded to a recording of Bethany singing *Twelve Days of Christmas*."

"Sorry, Sheriff. Bethany's officially on vacation, but she's still here, fussing and decorating. I'll go get her..."

"No, it's alright. It's you I wanted to talk to anyway."

"Oh," she said. "Of course." She sighed and sank down into the chair behind the desk.

"Not to worry – I still haven't got any response back on those dental records, so I'm not officially bearing bad tidings yet. I just wanted to find out how...you know...things. Are going on your end. I'm still concerned that your kids and their spouses aren't safe if that person in the Yellow House really is an impostor."

"I can assure you the impostor has been sent packing." She spoke quietly to prevent anyone overhearing through the still-open office door. "Um. I can give you more details if you want..."

"You sound like you'd rather not, though."

"I'm fairly confident you can handle the truth, Dunn. I'm just not sure how you're going to be able to put it into your report and still keep your job."

"Alright, well, look. If your family's alright, that's what matters for now. We can talk about the rest of it when the time comes. I'll be stopping by the party tonight anyway. With any luck – I mean, if you can call it luck – I might have some news from Raleigh by the time I get there."

"See you tonight, then." She pressed the disconnect button absently without remembering to say goodbye. Her family was not really alright, she knew. It was just that no sheriff in the world was empowered to help them with what was wrong.

She stared out the window at the falling snow. Her children and their significant others had probably been making remarks since breakfast, over eggnog and vegetarian holiday snacks, about how long it was taking Wes to return this time. Rosheen would be playing along, silently keeping her secret, while Kelleigh and Brandon would be exchanging dry jokes about how their father had always tended to create his own schedule anyway. Kelleigh, she was sure, would be laughing about it on the outside but inwardly starting to wonder if he actually had any intention of returning at all.

Cradling the telephone receiver against her stomach, she laid her head on the desk and groaned. She knew the real Wes, despite his faults, would have made it back in time to spend Christmas with his children. She had no idea what she would do when the sheriff could no longer hold off telling everyone who the body really was. That would be hard enough, under any circumstances. But on top of that she had no idea how she could explain why Wes had seemed to be with them even though his body had been found two days prior. She considered leveraging the common ghost-story trope about the dearly departed paying a final visit to its loved ones before crossing over...

Sitting up at last, she slammed the receiver back into its cradle.

"Fuck this for a game of soldiers!"

She dug her cell phone out of her purse and scrolled through her contacts to Kelleigh's number. She wished she hadn't let Rosheen convince her to conceal the truth to begin with. She was going to have to tell her children about her own strange, new life someday anyway, about everything that had changed for her since she'd come to Woodley. Brandon had been around Rosheen long enough that he would probably take the whole faerie part of it in stride. Kelleigh not so much – not at first, anyway – while Gordon would gently and kindly attempt to convince Kelleigh to put her mother in a home.

Whatever the case, there was no explanation she could give them for what had happened to Wes that wouldn't ruin their Christmas, this year and for many years to come.

The call went straight to voice mail, giving her a temporary reprieve. She left a terse "Let's meet for coffee. Call me back; love you!" message and jammed the phone into her too-small pocket so she'd be sure to have it on her when Kelleigh returned her call. Then she turned her attention to the next problem on her Christmas Eve agenda: her computer.

28 – Turning It Off and Back On Again

merald<< Hey, Cally, Merry Almost Christmas!

Emerald<< When's the last time you saw Georgie?

Cally wasn't sure, but she would have to think about it later, because the disquieting dialog boxes from last night now cascaded from the top left to the bottom right of her screen. Minimizing the chat window, she Alt+tabbed through them, careful not to click "OK" again in case they were a virus, even though it was probably already too late. The text became more alarming as she progressed.

"I need your help."
"Where are you?"
"This is not very much fun at all!"
"Can you even see these messages?"
"I'm afraid I've really messed up this time."

"Damn!" she said, and "Damn!" again as she read each one. Christmas or not, she was a writer and she needed a working computer. Hoping her novel in progress had not already been lost, she pulled her phone back out of her pocket, wondering if Luke's shop was even open today.

But Motherboard Pizza wasn't listed in her phone. She had always just walked there, before, whenever she needed pizza or technical advice. "Bethany!" she called out across the Hall. "Do you

146

have Luke's cell number?" If anyone knew it by heart, Bethany would, but the off-duty receptionist was singing loudly in the parlor (*White Christmas*, it sounded like) and did not reply.

She decided to just look it up on the web. If her web browser still worked, anyway. But before she could open the browser the chat icon blinked to let her know Emerald had sent another message. She sighed and clicked to open the chat program.

Emerald<< Have you seen George?

Emerald<< Because I have - - and I think he's upset about something

Cally>> Damn. Em, I don't really have bandwidth for his antics right now.

Cally>> And on top of everything, my computer is still acting up.

Emerald<< Well that's the thing

Emerald<< Is it still giving you those strange help messages?

Cally>> Yes. I'm going to have to take it to Luke. Why?

Emerald<< Because George is saying the same sorts of things

Emerald<< I've never seen him like this before

Emerald<< He keeps popping in and out of the background saying Help Me and I Don't Like This and things like that

Cally>> Background?

Emerald<< It's hard to explain

Emerald<< He has always been able to talk to me but he doesn't need a keyboard like you do

Emerald<< Normally I see and hear him kind of floating in the background

> **Emerald<<** But this time he's just a bunch of static
>
> **Emerald<<** And he sounds a bit panicky

Cally was starting to feel a bit panicky, herself. Had whatever was wrong with her computer begun to affect Emerald, too? She started her web browser, relieved to find it working properly, and browsed to her favorite search engine to look up Luke's number.

Her relief had been premature. The search engine was, without any input from her, conducting search after search on what seemed to be completely random topics, from rock music to world travel to grunge fashion. She didn't even have time to type in her own search terms before the browser would refresh to yet another screen full of results on a completely different topic. Not taking the time to swear, she quickly shut the browser down. Just as it disappeared from her screen, though, she realized the seemingly random searches did seem to have a pattern.

Pausing with her hands on the keyboard, she took a deep breath.

> **Cally>>** I think I know what's going on.
>
> **Emerald<<** For heaven's sake what? He just asked me what day it is
>
> **Emerald<<** He says he's afraid he's missed Christmas

In the upper left of her monitor, another series of dialog boxes began to cover the chat window.

"What day is it?"
"Cally I don't want to miss Christmas!"

Cally shook her head.

> **Cally>>** Em, I think our Georgie has found a way to explore the internet, like he's always

wanted to do.

Cally>> I suspect he was spying on me the other night when I rebooted the modem. I think he got into the internet through there.

Cally>> And I think he's beginning to realize he's not as clever as he thought! I'll be back in a minute or ten...

She took her shortcut via the spiral stair to her room, and from there dashed out into the upstairs hallway. Over the gallery railing she could see Ignacio removing the chairs from the dining room and taking them into the parlor, while Katarina turned the table into a buffet-line with chafing dishes and brightly-colored bowls all down its length. Not pausing to wave, she hurried to the little electrical closet across the hall from the Azalea room.

"Prepare to have your internet access revoked, Georgie." She reached into the dusty mass of tangled cables and switched off the power strip. As the little lights slowly faded from the modem and router, she turned around and looked down the length of the hall. Nothing but a row of closed white doors and framed pictures of southern botanicals met her gaze. She slowly counted to ten, as Ignacio had taught her.

She counted again, hoping she'd done the right thing and had not just switched off all hope of ever getting her ghost friend back from where he'd gone. She counted to thirty this time, just to be sure.

As she started her fourth count, turning reluctantly around to switch the equipment back on, she saw movement out of the corner of her eye. At the other end of the hall, a shadow seemed to be blocking the light of the green-shaded lamp on the butler's desk. She left the closet door open and ran the length of the hallway.

There was a ghost there, but it was only Doctor Boojums, paws curled under his chest as he settled down on top of the desk for a long winter's nap.

"Oh, buddy," she murmured softly to him. "I wonder if you can help?" The ghost cat didn't open his eyes, but his ear flicked as if he might be listening. "You've helped me before, Boo. Can you lead me to our George?"

"No need," said a voice behind her. "I'm right here!"

She spun around, flinging out her arms and nearly falling forward onto her face when her embrace encountered nothing. She didn't even care that he laughed at her as she stumbled and turned back around.

"I thought we'd lost you!" She realized Katarina might hear her shouting, over the gallery railing, but at the moment she didn't care.

George stopped laughing and his face grew sober. He was dressed rather soberly, as well, in a pinstriped suit and tie. "I thought you'd lost me, too," he admitted, nodding. "I thought the internet would be a fun way to travel. But there's so much of it..." He gazed past her shoulder, past the wall behind her. "So much, it goes on and on, branching this way and that. And it's so full of... Oh, Cally, not everything out there is fun, or interesting, or even nice at all. And I didn't know how to get back. It just kept going on, and on and on!"

He returned his gaze to her face, then, eyes wide and glittering with spectral tears. "I didn't mean to... Cally, you were right! You were right to be worried about me going out there!"

"I have never been so sorry to be right," she said, forgetting again and reaching out to take his hands. She stopped just before her own hands went through them. "But you're back now, and that's what matters.

"Except for one thing. You must promise me you'll never do that again!"

His usual sunny smile returned as if it had never been gone. "No need to promise! I will never try that again. Cally, what day is it? Have I missed Christmas?"

"You have not. It's Christmas Eve. It's almost time for the party. I wish you could smell the tacos." The deep breath she took, however, was not to inhale the aroma of Katarina's cooking, but an attempt to expel some of the tension from her body. "And George, I have a present for you."

"Great! You know what would make a great present? If you would make me the main character in one of your books!"

"Maybe someday," she waffled. "You can find this present

in the parlor. It's in the basket on the mantelpiece above the hearth. Behave yourself and don't disturb any of the guests who might have started to arrive."

His face lit up with excitement but he said, "I'll need you to carry my *zemi* into the parlor for me, please. You know I can't..."

"It is your *zemi*," she said, watching to see understanding dawn in his face, but her phone chose that moment to chime in with Kelleigh's ringtone. "Sorry, George," she said. "I don't want to, but I really ought to take this."

W e're on the porch!" Kelleigh laughed. "Oh! Never mind. Bethany just opened the door for us. Now we're in the living room... what? Bethany says it's called the parlor. Where are you? Let's get this party started!"

Relieved but aware it was only another reprieve, Cally restarted the modem then went back through the Dogwood Room, taking the spiral stair down to her office. Apparently Ignacio had managed to make Cally's MP3 player work with Bethany's stereo because she could hear, as she reached the bottom step, strains of Christmas music that had been recorded fewer than fifty years ago. She stopped at the desk to put her phone into the drawer, and typed a quick message to let Emerald know both George and her computer were now alright.

Through the office window she could see fat, white flakes still drifting down. Several party guests (she thought she recognized Jud Thornton from the hardware store among them) were approaching the house along the walkway Ignacio had swept clear. On the far side of the fence the three horses – black, white, and chestnut – kicked up their heels and cavorted like reindeer in the white meadow.

She was in no mood for a party, but she straightened her clothing, ran her fingers through her hair, and closed the door behind her as she stepped into the Hall. Several wrapped gifts had already been placed on the desk next to the glittering tinsel tree. Most of them, she noted, were distinctly bottle-shaped.

The sleigh bell on the front doorknob jangled as Jud, along with the two young proprietors of the Wyrd Systers Books and Gifts Shoppe, entered laughing and brushing snow from their hair. They greeted Cally cheerfully and hung their jackets on the already-laden coat rack; Jud placed another wrapped bottle on the desk. Cally returned what she hoped sounded like sincere season's greetings and followed them into the parlor.

In front of the north-facing picture window Kelleigh and Gordon, Brandon and Rosheen, all wearing red and green sweaters and holding glasses of wine, stood gazing out at the front yard. They looked like a vignette out of a Dickens novel, Cally thought, gathered like that against the backdrop of falling snow, but she also noted how all of them except Rosheen seemed to be watching the walkway, waiting for someone else to arrive.

"Hey, Mom!" Kelleigh turned from the window to give her a hug. "Bethany introduced us to Ignacio and Katarina when we came in, but who is *that*?" She gestured with her wineglass to where Doc stood next to the Christmas tree, apparently trying to help Bethany hang a green glass globe on a high branch. "Do I sense a December romance in the air?"

Despite her mood, Cally couldn't help smiling at that. "I think you might be right," she had to admit. "You generally are, about these things."

She exchanged hugs with the rest of her family, her shoulders tense as she waited for one of them to bring up the fact that Wes was not with them, but they merely resumed looking out the window at the walkway.

The sun had already gone behind the house, casting a rectangular shadow across the white lawn. Another group of guests was coming up the porch steps. Cally recognized Merv Arkwright, grinning broadly as he stamped snow off his shoes. He was accompanied by Andi from the coffee shop and her son Curtis but Nell, trailing in their wake, had turned back to have a quick chat with the horses on the other side of the fence.

"Yoo-hoo, we're in here!" Bethany waved across the parlor to the newcomers as they entered. Then she handed her still-unhung ornament to Doc. "Here, I give up. You do it!" she laughed. "I'm going to go fetch a tray of hors d'oeuvres. We're going to need something to tide us over until the tacos are ready!" She ran blushing from the room.

"Nice try, Doc," Brandon laughed as Doc hung up the

ornament himself, but the silver-haired gentleman didn't seem discouraged.

"It's good timing, actually." He watched until Bethany had disappeared into the back hall, then reached into his jacket. Winking, he pulled out a large, pink bow affixed to the top of a tiny, wrapped package. "I needed a chance to set this out."

"Oh!" Nell, entering the house at last, ran to his side with her coat still on. "You figured out what to put in that cute little box!"

Doc shook his head. "Not quite. But I made a wish! The right thing will be inside when she opens it."

Watching him tuck the bright gift into the branches, Cally managed not to say, "Doc, you've got to be kidding!" She mustered an encouraging smile, hoping his faith was not misplaced. Opening an empty box, regardless of its cuteness, might give Bethany exactly the opposite of his intended message.

By the time Bethany returned, she was wearing a much nicer dress than she'd been wearing when she'd left. More guests arrived, many of whom Cally did not recognize though they all seemed to know who she was. None of them, she noted, were dressed as Santa. Bethany made introductions where necessary while Ignacio described the list of available drinks. Nell encouraged everyone to choose ornaments from the bowl on the console table to hang on the tree. Many denizens of Woodley swarmed around Rosheen, congratulating her on her pregnancy and telling her she looked like she was glowing. Cally gave up, for the moment, any attempt to pull her family aside to speak to them in private. She still didn't know what she would say, anyway.

30 –   The Tacos Are Not Ready Yet

As the light faded outside, the aroma of Mexican seasonings began to overpower the fresh fir and rum punch fragrances of the parlor. Few guests actually sat in the many chairs Ignacio had brought from the dining room and Ian's study. They all stood, instead, talking in small groups and glancing surreptitiously over the rims of their drinks toward the back hall.

"It smells even better than Brandon's cooking in here," Kelleigh said. "And that's saying something!"

When Katarina appeared in the parlor doorway, the guests surged toward her as if they might stampede.

"*Calma por favor!*" She held up both hands and laughed. "You should know, after all these years. The tacos will not be ready until nightfall!" The party, as a body, turned toward the front window. Ignacio had switched on the porch light, but it was still not completely dark outside.

"How can one of the shortest days of the year be so damn long?" Jud Thornton lamented.

"Maybe this'll help y'all survive until the tacos are ready." Luke had arrived, and was standing just inside the door with a large pizza-warmer in his arms. "Pine-needle aged cheddar on sourdough focaccia with smoke-cured Christmas ham!" he called into the parlor.

Saluting him with a brandy glass, Doc called back, "Young man, even your fancy excuses for pizza can't compete with Kat's tacos!"

"It'll get eaten, though. You watch." Luke inclined his head toward the stereo, which was playing *Grandma Got Run Over by a Reindeer*. "But I think someone ought to put on some real Christmas music before Ian and Sofie join us!" He continued through the Hall, carrying his pizza into the dining room.

Cally hurried to the back of the parlor. As she pressed the MP3 player's skip button, Kelleigh appeared at her side.

"You don't have a drink, Mom!"

"I'll get one in a minute. I think. Listen, Kelleigh..."

"Listen, Mom..." Kelleigh began at the same time, and then laughed. "I have a feeling we're about to say the same thing! Okay, I'll go first. I just want you to know, I won't let it upset me if Dad doesn't show up. There was always the chance he wouldn't."

"Oh, sweetheart, I don't think that's true."

Kelleigh made a dismissive gesture with her glass. "He was acting really strange the whole time he was at Brandon's house. I think all this family stuff was making him feel trapped, and he lit out for the hills."

Cally knew better than to believe the laughter in her daughter's voice, or the smile plastered across her face. "Let's go into my office for a minute," she said, wondering how she might subtly invite Brandon to join them without attracting everyone else's curiosity.

"Really, I'm fine, Mom. Don't worry about it. Anyway, he still might turn up. Oh, look who's here!" She nodded toward the window, where they could see Ben ascending the porch steps with a bent figure clinging to his arm. "Is that his mother?"

"His sister." Cally answered over her shoulder as she dashed back across the room to the Hall. Katarina was there ahead of her, still wearing an apron over her Christmas-colored festival dress. Flinging open the door she cried out, "Brigid and Bennet Dawes!" by way of both greeting and announcement. "I'm so glad you could make it. Merry Christmas!"

"Blessed Yule to you, too," Bree muttered. "Here." Shrugging off her coat, she handed it to Ben and stumped past Cally into the parlor.

"I can't believe you convinced her to come!" Katarina said to Ben. "She's only ever been here for funerals, before." She turned to Cally. "Will you please find out what she'd like to drink? I still have a few last-minute things to do. And..." She fished in her apron pocket as she bustled out onto the porch. "I need to put out the carrots for Santa's reindeer!"

"For Errin and Mima, is how it will probably turn out," Ben said quietly as he sought places to hang Bree's coat and his own on the now heavily covered rack beside the door. He had a bemused look on his face when he turned around to take Cally's hand. "It feels so strange to be inside right now, rather than out by the fence. How are you holding up?"

She could only shrug. She honestly didn't know. Turning, she led him into the parlor, where Rosheen hurried from the window to throw her arms around him. "Merry Christmas, Father! I'm so glad you could come!"

Cally thought she saw them both wipe the corners of their eyes, but her own eyes were on her children, watching this scenario with sad smiles on their faces.

"I'll go get Bree her drink," she said, but Ignacio, carrying carafes of wine and brandy, had already served her and topped up everyone else's drinks, as well. Tapping the side of a decanter with a spoon, he directed their attention to the rear of the room where, to the tune of *Good King Wenceslas*, Ian May could be seen slowly emerging from the back hall with Sofie on his arm. Merv Arkwright put a brandy glass into his free hand, and this the old gentleman held high as he stepped into the parlor.

"Esteemed guests." Ian May beamed at all the assembled faces. "Merry Christmas, Happy Holidays, and Blessed Everything Else!" The esteemed guests all raised their glasses in cheery agreement.

Ian, Cally noted as he helped Sofie sit down in one of the wing chairs flanking the fireplace, was not dressed up as Santa Claus, though he was wearing a green tie with a pattern of dancing elves on it. Reluctantly, she eliminated him at last from her suspect list of possible Santas for the evening. Still, she thought, the old couple did resemble a Christmas card vignette of Mr. and Mrs. Claus in their matching chairs on either side of the cheerfully crackling fire.

Sofie seemed relaxed and in good spirits, but everyone knew not to crowd her or overwhelm her with greetings. "It's snowing!" she announced to the room in general. "I wish every Christmas, you know, for it to snow the next Christmas. But this year I am going to wish for..."

"Careful!" Doc called out to her. "If you tell, it might not come true."

"Oh, maybe for you!" She smiled coquettishly. "But I'm a special case."

Everyone present had to agree with that.

Then Sofie looked up past Cally's shoulder, and her smile turned into a wide grin. "Oh, look!" she said. "There's that pirate ghost!"

31 – Georgie Goes to a Party

Cally turned slowly to see George dressed in green trousers with red suspenders over the ugliest ugly Christmas sweater she had ever seen. A blinking Rudolf-nose necklace straight from the eighties hung from his neck. He didn't look a thing like a pirate; Cally had no idea how Sofie knew he'd been a pirate for part of his short life, but she didn't ask. She smiled and nodded just like everyone else in the room. Nobody tried to tell Sofie there was nothing there, but different tongues were held for different reasons.

George moved about the room like a flame, vanishing and reappearing in front of the windows, the tree, the new television set (which he regarded long and thoroughly with a furrowed brow.) When he spotted Cally he smiled and waved, then drifted across the room to stand beside Nell at the Christmas tree. Excusing herself, Cally joined them as nonchalantly as she could.

"Look what I got!" George was saying, pointing to his blinking reindeer necklace.

"Very cool," Nell answered quietly. "I had one just like it when I was in fifth grade." To nearby chatting guests, it looked like she was discussing the tree with Cally (or so Cally hoped.)

"That's where I got the idea!" George beamed at her, then tilted his head back, regarding the glorious hodgepodge of Christmas tree ornaments collected at Vale House over the years. Nell explained that many of these were gifts from bed and breakfast guests, including a series of lighthouses, each numbered with a different year, from longtime summer guests Celeste and William Iverson.

"I am so thankful to you, Cally," George said, almost in a whisper as he gazed up at the golden star on the top of the tree. "For helping me to see this."

159

She wasn't sure whether he was referring to the tree, or to the fact that he could now see he was free to go anywhere he wanted.

"I'm glad you're happy, Georgie," she replied softly. "But I hope you'll behave yourself."

"Always!" He laughed. "I'm going to go check out the kitchen now!" he added before he vanished.

32 – The Tacos are Ready

Katarina appeared in the doorway and took off her apron. Apparently this was the traditional signal for "the tacos are ready," because the guests began to surge toward the back hall – the shortest way to the dining room.

"Don't overfill your tortillas!" Katarina called after them. "Just make another one, if you want more fillings!"

"I'll get plates for Ian and Sofie," Cally volunteered.

"What about you?"

"I could ask you the same, Kat."

Katarina laughed. "I've been nibbling all day!"

"And you've been standing all day, too," Ignacio pointed out. "Sit down and put your feet up, now!" Ignacio did not take his own advice, but began helping guests find seats as they returned with laden plates. Nobody had heeded Katarina's advice, either, about overfilling their tortillas. Cries of dismay mingled with laughter each time Exploding Taco Syndrome threatened to ruin someone's Christmas sweater.

As Cally set plates of properly-filled (she hoped) tacos and gourmet pizza on the tea tables beside Sofie's and Ian's chairs, Ignacio finally managed to press a wine glass into her hand. He nudged her with his elbow and nodded meaningfully: Ian had raised his own glass to propose a toast.

"To loved ones, past and present, gathered or scattered, everyone's and everywhere!"

She drank thoughtfully to this, looking across the room at her son and daughter. They stood with Rosheen and Gordon in their own little group next to the tree. Snow fell gently in the picture window behind them as they nibbled at their tacos and tried to conceal their glances toward the front door, where the person they

161

were hoping might appear would almost certainly not appear, not that night, nor ever again.

Ian drained his glass. Merv took it from him and replaced it with a full one, ready to propose the second of many toasts that would be proposed that night. Bottles were brought in from the Hall and unwrapped.

Even Bethany sat down at last and began to nibble daintily at the plate of food Doc handed her. Cally thought she looked a little flushed around the cheeks and neck, though she couldn't tell whether that was from the wine or from whatever it was Doc leaned over her chair to whisper into her ear.

She was starting to feel a little flushed, herself, and breathless as if the chatting guests and the fire in the hearth were consuming all the oxygen in the room. When Ben returned to the room with a plate for Bree, she laid a hand on his arm. "I guess I'd better go find out if these tacos are all they're cracked up to be," she said. "I'll be right back." Then she fled into the dining room.

33 – The Sheriff Arrives

She didn't really want to eat tacos – she didn't really want to eat anything – but the rush of guests filling their plates had subsided. She could breathe more easily as the last of them dabbed far too much salsa and guacamole onto their plates and went back to the parlor. Taking a plate from the sideboard, she stood beside the tortilla warmer for several minutes and tried to work the kinks out of her shoulders.

She had just decided she might try some of Luke's pizza when she heard the jingle of the sleigh bell on the front door handle. Turning to look into the Hall, she saw Dunn Mahon shutting the door behind himself, stomping snow from his shoes onto the mat.

"Sheriff!" she heard someone in the parlor call out (it sounded like Merv Arkwright.) "Nice to see you in civilian clothes for a change!"

The sheriff waved and grinned as he brushed snow off his jacket, but he had spotted Cally in the dining room. "I'll be right with you gentlemen," he called back into the parlor. "The tacos smell like heaven! Pour me some of whatever you're having."

When he came into the room, he stood beside Cally and picked up a plate as if to fill it with food, but then he stood still, holding the plate in front of his chest as he might have held his hat, had he been in uniform.

"I'm afraid I still have one last bit of official business to conduct," he said softly. She put down her own plate and nodded, waiting without speaking because she already knew what he was going to say. "The report came back from Raleigh, and they have positively matched the body to the dental records of your ex-husband. I'm sorry."

She let out a sigh. "I knew they would," she said, leaning

163

both hands on the table. "It's just, I'm not looking forward to having to tell my kids, on Christmas Eve, that their father will not be joining them tonight. Or ever again. But if I don't tell them until after Christmas, they'll be even more upset when they find out I hid it from them. Oh, God, Dunn. Could you just, I don't know, pretend you haven't told me yet?"

"I'm starting to understand why Ian never really included me in his little in-group, here. He knew all the lying I'd have to do would compromise my job."

"Sorry, Dunn."

"There's nothing for you to be sorry about." He put his free arm around her shoulders. "I've done my duty. I've delivered the information to you. What you choose to do with it is none of my business.

"Maybe you should have some tacos," he suggested. "Ignacio's salsa might clear your head."

She laughed in spite of herself. "Maybe in a little while."

"Won't be any left in a little while!" He spread four tortillas on his plate, dabbing just a little bit of filling into the middle of each one, the way Katarina had tried to instruct everyone else. As he moved along the table to the bowls of chopped cilantro and onions, other guests began returning to the dining room for seconds.

"Even Bree likes the tacos." Ben joined them beside the table. "And she doesn't like anything! I suspect I'll be fetching and carrying for her for hours." Cally had to grin at that, because he looked like he was actually enjoying his evening of servitude.

When he spotted Cally's empty plate, though, his smile faded. "Are you alright?"

"I'm fine," she said, in the way one does when one wants to let someone know they are absolutely not fine. Grateful tears stung her eyes when he put Bree's plate down and wrapped his arms around her. "I think I know what I need to wish for now," she said into his chest.

"Don't worry." He kissed her hair. "You'll do the right thing. I know you will. You always do."

Feeling like a traitor, she gave him a smile as he turned to carry Bree's second serving into the parlor.

She stared awhile at the splendid array of food all along the table, but decided it was probably a bad idea to eat anything, let alone anything spicy, feeling as she was. As she carried her empty plate back to the sideboard, a chorus of cries went up in the parlor. It sounded a little more amazed, perhaps even confused, than the usual response to a toast. The people in the dining room rushed back to the parlor to see what was going on and Cally followed, thinking, "Georgie, what have you done now?"

George was there as she had suspected, facing the Christmas tree with his back to her. She could almost, but not quite, see the twinkling lights right through him. He was waving his arms like a conductor, while the lights on the tree blinked in perfect time to the Perry Como song playing on the stereo. All conversation in the room became a breathless hush as lights pulsed from the top to bottom of the tree in synch with the lyrics. Everyone was staring agape at the tree, except Nell who was grinning at George.

When the song ended, so did the special effects. George turned around to face his audience, holding his arms out at his sides and bowing deeply. "Merry Christmas!" he said as Nell applauded.

"Do it again!" Sofie cried out, but George disappeared and did not perform an encore.

"Well, now," said Ian. "Well, now... Wasn't that something?"

"Probably something to do with that newfangled music player thingy Cally talked me into using." Bethany let out a snort and shook her head, but her eyes were as big as saucers.

Doc patted her on the shoulder. "Or maybe it's a sign Santa is getting near. It's just about time, you know." He held up his brandy glass in a salute to the wrong entity, but he wasn't far wrong about the time. The clock on the mantel read twenty minutes to midnight.

34 –   Santa Arrives

So where's Santa?" Cally asked as she joined Ben where he stood with Jud and Merv behind Bree's chair.

"Don't worry, he'll be here at midnight!" Bethany wiped her mouth and folded her napkin. "The stroke of midnight. He's very punctual!" She stood and began collecting everyone's empty plates. Doc followed and helped her carry them out through the back hall.

Talk and chatter throughout the room grew more animated except, Cally noticed, in the corner where Brandon and Kelleigh stood silently watching out the window. Her hand rose of its own volition to press against her heart. By the time Bethany and Doc returned, everyone had stood up and was looking, glasses in hand, at the clock on the mantel. Cally had left her empty glass in the dining room but she joined the crowd in watching the fireplace. Was Santa really going to come plunging out of the chimney, scattering burning logs with his big, black boots? The brass bells of the antique clock began to chime, deeply and sonorously, one clear stroke for each hour.

Katarina pointed at the parlor's fancy tray ceiling as a clatter arose on the roof above them. It sounded more like an eighteen-wheeler braking roughly to a stop than eight tiny reindeer. Sofie applauded, and a cold draft blew through the room, putting out the fire in the hearth.

"To your health!" said a man who stood among the guests. He seemed to have been standing there all along, glass raised with all the others, but Cally knew he had not been there a moment ago. Ennilangr, the big-boned, blond-ponytailed delivery driver, was not a person anyone would miss seeing in even the biggest crowd. He was wearing a red plaid lumberjack shirt with a collar trimmed in

166

golden fleece.

As everyone acknowledged his toast with a merry cheer, the fire in the hearth leapt up blazing again as if it had never been out. Further toasts were proposed. Merv went out to the Hall to fetch another of the wrapped bottles from the desk.

Ennilangr strode (someone like him could never merely walk) to the fireside to shake Ian's hand. When he bent to kiss Sofie's cheek, she blushed and smiled directly into his eyes, then reached a hand up to whisper something into his ear. Giving her a nod and a wink, he reached into the basket on the mantel. One by one he removed the little paper scrolls, read them, and tossed them into the fire.

"Well, there's our official Woodley Santa Claus." It was Brandon, making his way through the crowd to Cally's side. "Merry Christmas, Mom." He gave her a warm hug. Kelleigh and Rosheen followed. Rosheen said nothing but, as she held Cally in a long embrace to hide her tears in Cally's shoulder, Cally could feel that Rosheen's pregnancy was finally becoming obvious.

"How did Ennilangr get to be Santa Claus, anyway?" Cally muttered to no one in particular.

She'd meant it rhetorically, but Ben answered. "It's a long story. Several long stories, overlapping and intertwining."

"Just like all stories," she said. "Just like all the roads."

He smiled and squeezed her hand, watching the scene next to the fireplace along with everyone else. Cally thought she recognized, when Ennilangr removed it from the basket, Ben's wish. As he untied the ribbon around it, she had to look away. She watched the side of Ben's face instead. His quiet smile was one of both hope and trepidation, and Cally felt even worse for what she was about to do.

Letting go of Ben's hand, she made her way across the room to stand on tiptoe behind the big-boned trucker. "You don't look a thing like Santa," she whispered up to his ear.

When he turned to look at her, his eyes twinkled like ice. "And you don't look a thing like a Faerie Queen," he pointed out.

"That's because I'm not one."

He didn't say anything, but stood silently regarding her. She jabbed a knuckle at a tear stinging the corner of her eye. "I'm ready to make my wish now," she said at last.

"I thought you might be."

She looked across the room to Ben, smiling his silent promise back at her. He was hoping, she knew... No, he was believing. He was believing she was about to make the same wish he had made. Regret squeezed the breath right out of her chest as she realized she was about to throw away not only her own wish but his as well.

"Step outside with me," Ennilangr said. "Tell me your wish before you think better of it."

35 – Sympathy for the Devil

I t's a bit unorthodox. I don't know if you can do it."

Ennilangr stood below her, on the walk at the base of the porch steps. He cast two shadows across the snow: one from the porch light behind her and another, stretching in a different direction, from the moon. Fat, soft flakes fell all around him. At least four inches had accumulated, re-covering the walkway, softening all the angles and edges of the steps, the fence, the barn. The front yard swept straight out into the meadow in one solid swath of white interrupted only by colorful reflections from the lights along the fence.

"It's like they've been telling you," he said. "As long as it does not interfere with the free will of any other person, your wish can be anything."

"Even bringing someone back from the dead?"

He didn't seem at all taken aback by this. He merely nodded and said, "As long as they are willing."

Her hand swept snow from the porch railing as she carefully descended the steps to stand beside him. She forced herself to speak past the lump in her throat.

"Then I wish for my children's father to be able to keep his promise to spend Christmas with them."

He nodded. "So be it."

Reaching out to take her hand, with his other hand he produced a glittering object from his pocket. It felt heavy, smooth and cold when he nestled it into her palm. "Go to where he was last alive." He nodded over his shoulder, down the slope of the white lawn to the pond glittering in the distance. "You'll know what do." He bowed to kiss her cheek. "Merry Christmas." And then, without another word, he turned and went back into the house.

169

She stood alone in the moonlight watching him go. The air was so silent and still, she could hear the soft hiss of snowflakes hitting the ground all around her. It was already filling in her footprints on the steps, but not before she noticed that her own footprints were the only ones there. A shudder, which had nothing to do with the cold, went through her. When the front door closed behind Ennilangr, she thought it sounded like the slamming of a tomb.

She looked at the object in her hand. It was a snow globe. A tiny, white antebellum house glowed in its center amid snowflakes swirling like fireflies. Upon its roof stood a miniature sleigh, but instead of eight tiny reindeer, only two beasts were harnessed to it. They appeared, to the best she could make out, to be golden rams. Sighing, she tucked the globe into her jacket. Then she turned away from Vale House and headed down the hill, past the barn toward the pond.

The snow stopped just after she passed the barn. The ground here, she noted with some consternation, was completely bare underfoot, and the cold was now much sharper – raw like it had been two days before. She could no longer see the colorful lights along the meadow fence.

The backs of her shoulders began to tingle. She suddenly knew without looking that, should she turn around, she would see more bare ground behind her, all the way back to Vale House and beyond. She did not turn around.

The air was so bitter she half expected her breath, pluming white in front of her, to freeze solid and fall to the ground. Clutching her jacket closed across her chest, she ducked under the birch branches to follow the moonlit path around the pond. Shimmering ice rimmed the shallows around the banks, but the moon's reflection rippled across the black water in the center. No fishing trawler lay grounded on the western bank.

She walked around the place where Ian's boat should have been and turned to approach the northern bank. Looking up through the bare birches and young willows, she could see ahead to the twinkling lights of the houses along Bells Road. The full glory of ten pounds of Christmas lights per linear foot of roofline lifted her heart a little.

"Merry Christmas," she breathed to the festive scenario, and then she saw him. A tall, lanky man had stepped off the shoulder of Bells Road. He was walking across the field toward her, crouched over a small flashlight shining dimly upon a piece of paper in his hand.

"Wes!"

She heard her own voice call out to the man, but she had not spoken. She turned her head to look toward the sound just as Wes did. There, standing in the field next to the north bank of the pond, she saw herself waving and smiling.

Her stomach flipped, and she grasped the slim trunk next to her to ground herself in reality. *You've seen this sort of thing before*, she reminded herself sternly. Time was just a utility to faeries and other immortals. She had seen them alter it for their own purposes several times. She had even witnessed previous iterations of herself doing things she'd already done. Naturally, she had deep reservations about messing around with time, but this was different.

As she watched her own cheerful face, seemingly untroubled by the cold, wearing the same clothes she'd been wearing three days ago, she knew she had not stood there on that night. She was absolutely certain, she insisted to herself, that she had never stood under the moon at the edge of any pond waving cheerily to Wes Edwards, not three nights ago, not ever.

Wes ran across the field toward her other self calling "Cally!" He stopped a few feet short, arms out, panting deep breaths of frosty air. Cally thought he looked like he was considering whether or not to hug the apparition. Her instincts told her to interfere, but she wasn't sure whether that would make the situation better or worse.

"Please," Wes called out. "I just want to... I mean, I know it's too late for us. I just want to try to make things up to Kelleigh and Brandon. I promise to stay out of your way but... Cally, it's almost Christmas and... and I'm freezing my ass off!"

"It's alright," she watched herself say. "We were all worried about you." The other Cally stepped forward and put an arm around Wes's shoulders. "Everyone's waiting for you in the house. Go on!"

171

It turned and waved with one arm in a wide gesture toward the pond.

But there, where the pond should have been, stood Vale House in all its brightly-lit, welcoming splendor like an icy Fata Morgana. The illusion was so well-constructed Cally could even hear happy voices and Christmas music emanating from it.

"Go on in and get warm," said Faux-Cally. "Everything will be fine. After all, it's Chris... Chr.. a holiday!"

As she watched herself struggle to say the word "Christmas," Cally saw a flash of yellow teeth in the moonlight.

"Eladha!" she spat in a burst of frosty breath. "So that's how you did it!"

The Formorian really had not been lying when he'd insisted he hadn't broken faerie law by killing Wes outright, or by otherwise interfering with his free will. He had merely used glamour to trick a gullible human into stepping into the pond – it was the oldest fae-trickery trope in the book.

Wes smiled through chattering teeth at his unexpected benefactor. "Thank you, Cally. I owe you." He turned and started toward the illusory Vale House.

Cally wondered what would happen if she should jump out of the shadows and call to him. Would the sight of two of her frighten him away completely? That, she thought, might not be such a bad option. It wasn't quite what she'd wished for, but it was better than having to tell her children their father was dead on Christmas Eve.

Even as she pondered her dilemma, she realized she had already begun stumbling forward through the underbrush. "Wes, stop!" she was shouting. "It's just a glamour!"

He didn't hear her, because her other self, turning swiftly to glare at her with snake-slit eyes, shouted over her words. "Hurry, Wes! I'll catch up with you in a minute!" Eladha called sweetly to Wes in her voice, but his gaze was locked on Cally, and his long, bare teeth glittered like knives. In a completely different voice which seemed almost to be speaking directly into her ear he hissed, "Be quiet! You're ruining everything!"

Cally heard ice crack under Wes's feet. She cupped her hands around her mouth to shout again, and then all semblance of her own face melted like moonlight from the face of her double. Eladha crouched to the ground, long arms reaching out to tear aside any underbrush that stood between him and Cally.

She ducked and rolled into a thicket of young willows next to the bank. Landing on hard, frozen mud, she felt the snow globe inside her jacket bruise her ribs. She pressed a hand over her mouth to stop herself crying out, but it didn't matter. When she looked up, Eladha was glaring down at her through the willows' bare branches.

Feeling as if she was moving in slow motion, she rose to her knees and drew the snow globe out into the moonlight. Ennilangr had told her she'd know what to do with it. She still wasn't sure she knew, but there was no time to wonder. Eladha, slashing through the thicket, leaned over her growling low in his throat. "If you don't stop interfering with every single..."

She threw the globe, not at Eladha but across the pond, straight into the midst of the glowing facsimile of Vale house. As it hit with a splash, the illusion of the house shattered in a shower of bright shards dropping soundlessly one by one into the water. Wes, halting suddenly, slipped on the ice and fell.

Eladha's mouth was still moving, his claws still plunging through the branches toward Cally but even as she rolled out of his reach she could only guess what he was trying to say. His voice seemed to spiral away like water down a drain. His visage followed, swept sideways like a swiftly turned page. Where he had stood, now snow drifted down between the branches.

Cally scrambled to her feet and looked back to the pond. Wes Edwards, on hands and knees, spluttered and slipped, struggling to stand up in three or four inches of water swirling with razor-thin shards of ice. Thick flakes of snow were falling softy all around him, covering the banks and bare trees in a blanket of moonlit white.

"What the hell?" he muttered, shivering and spitting out mud. "What the hell?"

Cally hurried through the snow to his side and fastened her hands on his jacket. Drawing him back from the water, she said "Not hell, but close."

"What was I... I could have sworn there was a house."

"It's alright," she said. "We're back in the present, now."

"Where am I?" He turned around and around where he stood. "I fell...I think I must have hit my head."

"You're alright. It was kind of a mirage." She quickly bent a few principles of physics to suit this poor explanation. "A temperature inversion because of the cold. The house is actually up there." She pointed up the hill to where Vale House – the real Vale House – twinkled warmly beyond the birches. "This way," she said, leading him by the arm the long way around the black water.

He was shivering violently; she practically had to drag him up the hill. The whole way, he blustered between chattering teeth about how he didn't want to make Christmas awkward for her and how he hadn't been able to find Woodley but a friendly stranger had come out of nowhere and drawn him a map and told him how to get there on foot and "I thought you didn't get snow in this part of the country?"

"We do sometimes," she oversimplified, helping him up the porch steps. "This is a ... different sort of place."

"Thank you," he said. "Not just for pulling me out of that swamp. Thank you for not turning me away. I really just want to spend Christmas with my kids."

She reached for the door handle. "Let's get you in out of the cold."

The sleigh bell jangled as she showed him, hunched over and shivering, into the Hall. Through the parlor door she could see Kelleigh turn to look, the sorrow on her face melting rapidly into wonder as she nudged Brandon's shoulder. Both of them put down their drinks and started toward the Hall, followed closely by Rosheen and Ben. Cally steered Wes to the Hall side of the fireplace and he sank to his knees before it, trembling hands extended toward the flames.

"Get yourself warm. I'll fix you a plate of tacos. Wes." In spite of his wet clothes, she bent to give him a hug. "I really am glad you're aliv... here."

The bell on the front door clanged again. She looked up to see Kelleigh and Brandon, with Rosheen close behind, hurrying toward Wes, but Ben was gone.

36 – The Other Shoe

He had to leave at midnight," Bree reminded her, not exactly kindly, but in tones more mellow than she usually used. Cally credited the rum punch everyone kept making sure to top up in her cup.

She wasn't reassured, though. She recalled that Ben had not, in fact, left at midnight. He had stayed to watch Santa-langr grant wishes. He'd been waiting to see if his own wish was going to come true. He'd been waiting to see if Cally had helped it come true by wishing the same thing.

But she hadn't.

She tried to tell herself she hadn't thrown away her shot. She'd done a good thing with it. The right thing. As she watched her children introduce their father to the others at the party, she knew she'd done the right thing. But she also knew she'd broken the heart of the man she loved – the man who loved her.

Knowing it was futile, she put her jacket back on and left the partygoers behind her as they began to exchange and open gifts. Of course she did not see Ben standing near the fence waiting for her. Why should he be? Sighing, she crossed the snowy lawn anyway, laying her arms on top of the colorful lights. Just a short distance away she could see the three horses, ebony, rosegold and silver in the moonlight, cavorting in the snow, pretending to ignore her. She wondered if she could convince one of them to carry her to Rianwynn's court, and she wondered if Ben would speak to her even if she did. She wished she could cry, but the tears were frozen inside her.

"Armadeur, where is my son?"

She jumped when the sharp voice erupted seemingly out of the darkness next to her elbow. Just on the other side of the fence

175

she saw a silver gown fluttering in the moonlight, green jewels flaming in a golden crown.

She had no strength for diplomacy. "How the hell should I know?" she asked the Faerie Queen.

Rianwynn stepped out of the nonexistent shadows, along with four armor-clad warriors. "Do not dare lie to me. He did not return to my court at midnight as instructed."

"Well, he's not here. Don't look at me like that. Do you think I'd be standing out here in the cold if I had him squirreled away in my bedroom?"

A snort of laughter came from one of Rianwynn's companions. Cally knew, by the flying mane of ruby hair as the warrior stepped away from the others, that it was Aileen.

"Your Majesty." Aileen did not approach, but bent to one knee, peering down into the snow. "I think he went this way." With one slender, white hand she described a line from the fence toward the eastern horizon.

"Of course he did," Cally muttered, more to herself than to any faerie.

"Where did he go, then?" Rianwynn, also, didn't seem to be talking to anyone but herself. "If he didn't go back to my country, he'll freeze to death out here. He's got too much human..."

Aileen stood and, still bent over the snow, walked slowly into the distance. Straightening suddenly, she turned and called over her shoulder. "His tracks end here."

Cally might have enjoyed seeing Rianwynn at a loss for words for once, but she suddenly thought she understood.

"Wait," she called to Aileen. "I think I know..." Ducking under the top rail, she slipped through to the other side of the fence. "I think I know where he went."

She ran along the faint indentations in the snow that must have been Ben's tracks, barely noticing that Aileen had not left any herself. The Faerie warrior stood frowning into the rolling, white distance where no tracks at all led.

"I know where he went," Cally said when reached Aileen's side. "And I know how to get there."

Aileen grinned conspiratorially at her. "Oho, so. He's been

teaching you how to see the real roads."

"There is no road here," Rianwynn said, appearing beside them as if the breeze had borne her there. "Neither mortal nor faerie."

"No, neither one," Cally agreed. "But I can see it anyway." She could, if she closed her eyes. If she looked with her heart. "It's a place he made, just for himself, and for me, even though he hadn't even met me yet, back then..." Eyes shut, she turned slowly, trampling a perfectly round hole into the snow. Behind her eyelids she could see paths flowing beneath her feet, crisscrossing and twisting. She didn't know where most of them led, but she recognized one she had followed once with Ben. In hue and tone it reminded her of a spring day, and it connected to many others...

She opened her eyes to meet Rianwynn's glower and said, "And it's inside of Faerie, so you can call off your International Incident."

"Could you find it again?" Aileen asked.

She nodded. She could find it the way she could find her way around Vale House in the dark. The way she could find her own heartbeat in a noisy room.

"Very well." Rianwynn signaled to her other soldiers. "We'll follow you, then."

"You can try, if you like." Cally closed her eyes again and stepped where her feet showed her to go. She turned again and saw the next crossing, shining in her imagination, and her heart knew which turn to take. "But you won't be able to. This is *his* place," she explained, even though she knew the faerie women, Vale House, and even the snow were no longer there. "His, and mine."

She opened her eyes at last when a warm, fragrant breeze caressed her face and hands. Above her, stars shone down through a bower of budding beech branches. Ben sat in the grass a short distance away from them with his back to her, gazing across the hills to the horizon. Even now a faint light shone there, like a distant city. He must have heard her footsteps, she thought, but he didn't turn his head at her approach.

She sank silently to her knees on the ground beside him. He still didn't turn his head, but she heard his trembling voice say, "I

177

can't. I can't do this."

She believed she knew what he meant, and she couldn't blame him. How could any man do this? To remain in a relationship that had no hope of ever being fulfilled, to go on living torn between two worlds where he could never truly be hers in either one of them, and she could never truly be his? She had no right to expect him to. She wanted to lay a hand on his shoulder, to ask him to turn and look at her, but she had no right to do that, either.

She knew she should say something, but everything she thought of seemed either too flip or too desperate. "I understand," was the best she could come up with and it sounded especially lame once she'd said it. Her heart felt like a rock in the center of her chest, but she forced herself to go on. "I understand. I promised you from the beginning that I was prepared to let you go when I had to. When the time came. I guess this is..."

He turned at last to look at her, and she was unable to continue speaking. The pain in his eyes reached out and wrapped palpably around her. She knew that pain was her doing – her own fault, for letting herself get involved with him in the first place. She had a sudden, clear memory of the first time they'd sat on this hilltop. It had been a sunny day, and it had been the first time, she recalled then, that she'd told him, "I'm not very good at not doing things I shouldn't do." It had been the first time they'd made love...

"I know what I'm supposed to do," he said, as if he'd heard her thoughts. "I'm supposed to stand up and walk away." He nodded toward the light in the distance. "I've always known I would have to, someday. I've always promised I would be able to. But I can't." Even as he spoke, he was reaching toward her. "I'm no great faerie hero." His arms slid around her, so warm she couldn't help but melt into them. "I'm just a man," he said into her hair. "And I can't do this. I can't walk away from you."

"Then don't." She pressed her face into his chest to hide her tears. "I'm so sorry. This is all my fault. We could have resolved this whole dilemma tonight. You believed that, and I almost did. But I threw away my wish, and yours with it."

"No." Gently, he pushed her back enough that she could see his face in the moonlight. "You did the right thing. You did exactly

178

what the woman I love would have done." He took her hand and pressed it over his heart. "There is no blame in here for you."

His blue eyes shone so steadily that she barely noticed the tears slipping from them. When she did, she felt her own thaw at last and run freely down.

"Well," she said at length, taking off her jacket and using its sleeve as a makeshift handkerchief. "I guess there's always next Christmas."

He grunted out a little, fake laugh. "I guess. Except now we've pretty much told one another our wishes, which means they can't come true even then."

Cally spat a detailed description of what the rules around wishing could do with themselves.

He laughed a real laugh, then. "Yes," he agreed. "Sideways." Taking the jacket from her, he turned it inside out and folded it on the grass behind them. Then he gave her a serious look. "We'll think of something," he said. "We will, if you believe we will."

"I believe," she promised, lying back on the makeshift pillow. "We'll think of something, in the morning."

December

25

Christmas Day

37 –   It's In Every One Of Us

The snow had stopped by the time they arrived at Vale House in the morning. Ignacio's swept walkway had been covered over sometime before it had stopped, but many fresh footprints led from the gateposts to the house. When Cally and Ben neared the front door, a familiar aroma of tacos filled the chilly air. Cally wondered if the Christmas party was still going on.

Apparently, however, it was a full Vale House Bed and Breakfast breakfast, in progress in the dining room. At the sound of the brass bell on the doorknob, the entire staff of Vale House, as well as a handful of guests, turned in their seats to cheer and wave as Cally and Ben entered.

"I'm sorry if I worried you all, disappearing like that last night." Cally rushed into the dining room with her jacket still on.

"We weren't worried." Kelleigh, seated with Gordon on the opposite side of the table, threw her a wink. "Mr. Dawes disappeared about the same time you did, so it was pretty easy to guess where you'd gone!"

Cally didn't think Kelleigh knew exactly where she'd gone, but she had the right basic idea.

The long dining table was nearly at capacity this morning, but a place had been left for Cally at Ian's left hand, with another empty place beside it for Ben. Katarina passed the coffee carafe as they sat down.

Ben said, "This smells wonderful, Kat. What is it?"

"It's called *migas*. It's what you do with leftover tacos!"

As Ben filled his plate, Cally squinted skeptically at what seemed to be a strata made with layers of eggs, leftover tortillas, and taco fillings.

"Don't worry. It's not too spicy!" Katarina assured her.

"I believe you, Kat. It's just I'm surprised there were enough leftover tacos to make it.

"Has anyone heard from Sheriff Mahon this morning?" she added as she served herself a small portion.

"Well, no." Bethany gave her a puzzled look. "He's probably on call today, but why would we have heard from him?"

"I was just checking to see if he..." She let out her breath, reassured that time was properly back on track and nobody (except possibly Ignacio, who was different that way) even remembered there had ever been a body in the pond. "I guess I was just making sure everyone made it home safely last night. Nobody fell through the ice into the pond on their way home or anything like that."

Everyone laughed. "Cally, you're such a Yankee!" Bethany said. "Ponds here don't ice over before January, if at all!" Ignacio nodded agreement at this, but he smiled sideways at Cally.

"Now, Ms. Chase." Ian spoke up softly from the head of the table. Cally thought the master of the house seemed unusually quiet this morning, probably due to all the toasts he'd drunk the night before, but he smiled bravely at Bethany. "You are supposed to be on vacation. Don't tell me you've come to work anyway."

Bethany blushed and took a deep swallow of coffee. "No, no," she blustered. "It's just... I just wanted to show everyone. What Doc gave me last night. Look at this!" She held up her hand with the ring-finger elevated.

"Oh, my, is that?" Katarina jumped up from her seat and ran around to Bethany's side of the table. Everyone else enthused various congratulations.

"Calm down," Bethany said. "It's not that kind of ring."

"Maybe not, but it *is* very nice." Cally reached across the table to take Bethany's hand. The ring was wrought of the deeply yellow kind of gold that was rarely seen anymore. Fine filigree tendrils of a redder shade of gold framed a large and colorful opal.

"That's a vintage piece," said Kelleigh. "I'm impressed!"

Nell smiled at Cally and winked. "Doc has good taste."

"He certainly does." Bethany had lowered her hand and was holding the ring close to her bosom as she gazed at it. "An altogether fine gentleman."

As Katarina went back around the table, she pointed out the

empty chair at the end. "Where's your dad?" she asked Kelleigh. "I made a special point last night of letting him know he was invited back for breakfast!"

Brandon, slathering extra salsa on top of his *migas*, answered. "We tried to rouse him when we left, but he begged us to let him sleep in. I don't know what he was up to all day yesterday, but whatever it was took the mickey out of him. He kept saying he couldn't believe it was Christmas day. He thought he'd been wandering around in the cold for three days or something – it was like something straight out of Scrooge."

Rosheen nodded. "He'll probably recover in time for at least one Christmas dinner. We're serving our dinner at noon. That way we can be here for the Vale House Christmas Dinner this evening, too." She laid a hand on Ben's arm. "What about you, Father? Will you be joining us?"

"Well, I..." He looked around the table. "I've always spent Christmas Day with Bree. Ever since I was, you know, much younger. It's the only day she doesn't open the store and we would have a quiet little supper together at the old homeplace." He looked from Rosheen to Cally and back again. "I'm sure she'd be delighted if you'd both join us."

Cally was pretty sure Bree would not be delighted with her crashing their private family meal, but Rosheen said, "I'll be there!"

"That's a lot of dinners!" Katarina laughed over the brim of her coffee cup. "Are you sure you're only eating for two, and not three? Or four!"

Rosheen shook her head and smiled patiently. It was Nell who explained in a serious voice, "It takes a lot of energy to raise a young Star."

"Mom," said Brandon, "I think you should go with Ben and Rosheen. Bree's a bit crotchety, but she has a heart of gold, deep down inside."

"Very deep down inside," Cally did not say out loud. "I'll think about it," she conceded. "But before we go anywhere, I want to take a little walk into town. I want to see what Woodley looks like covered in snow."

"Next year," Sofie piped up, "my Christmas snow is going

to be especially magical!"

"We'll spend all year looking forward to it!" Nell applauded as everyone else smiled and nodded. Cally wasn't sure she would be looking forward at all to an "especially magical snowfall" but she smiled and nodded anyway.

"Well." Cally stepped out through the little wooden gate at the rear of the Vale House grounds. Then she stopped where she was, unwilling to take another step and mar the pristine blanket of white before her. "Well, now. Isn't that something."

The sun had come out, and Main Street glittered in its light. Crystalline drifts like heaped diamonds softened the curbs so Cally could see little distinction between sidewalk and road. Porch steps and railings slumped lumpily down onto what looked like a single wide, pearly lawn stretching all the way along the opposite side of the street.

All the front doors remained quietly closed, railings absent their cats. Only the cheerful splotches of bright red bows interrupted the whiteness, lined up like bright guideposts along the frosted palisade all the way into town. The oaks marched alongside like rows of marble pillars, their ghostly and indistinct branches forming a vaulted ivory ceiling above the street. Not a single tire track, not a single footprint broke the alabaster sweep of the road itself. At the end of this hall of oaks, downtown Woodley was just a blur in the distance, more like a memory than an actual place.

As she gazed, barely breathing, a soft, fitful breeze began to rise at her back. It was neither cold nor warm, but every now and then, if it swirled through the oaks just so, wet, white clumps would lose their grip on the branches and fall with a thump into the street. The snow was already beginning to melt.

Playlist

Dear friends:

Here is a list of some of the songs from Cally's MP3 player, which Bethany played for the Christmas party. If you put these on your own player on shuffle, they will help you get into a very festive mood. At least, they certainly did for me!

Best of love and happiest of holidays, any time and everywhere,
Your faithful servant,
Guacanagarix

A Baby Just Like You - John Denver
Adeste, Fideles - Enya
Ave Maria - Celine
Away in a Manger - Celtic Woman
Bring a Torch, Jeanette, Isabella - Mannheim Steamroller
Canon in D Major - Minister
Canon in D Major - Anna Maria Mendieta
Canon in D Major - Gtrman
Carol of the Bells - Moya Brennan
Carol of the Bells - Trans-Siberian Orchestra
Christmas Eve /Sarajevo - Trans-Siberian Orchestra
Christmas Canon - Trans-Siberian Orchestra
Christmas in the Trenches - John McCutcheon
Coventry Carol - Narada
Deck the Halls - Bob Hope
Ding Dong Merrily on High - Celtic Woman
Do You Hear What I Hear - Bob Hope
God Rest Ye Merry, Gentleman - John Denver
Good King Wenceslas - Manheim Steamroller

Grandma Got Run Over by a Reindeer - Elmo & Patsy
Happy Christmas (War is Over) – *John Lennon*
Hark, The Herald Angels Sing - Vince Guaraldi Trio
Have Yourself A Merry Little Christmas - Frank Sinatra
I Believe in Father Christmas - Emerson, Lake & Palmer
It's In Every One Of Us - John Denver and the Muppets
Jesu, Joy of Man's Desiring - Celtic Woman
Journey of the Angels - Enya
Joy to the World! - Perry Como
Merry Christmas from the Family - Montgomery Gentry
O Come O Come Emmanuel - Enya
O Come, All Ye Faithful - Pentatonix
Oh, Holy Night - Ella Fitzgerald
Run, Run Rudolph – Chuck Berry
Silent Night - Bing Crosby
Silver Bells - Bob Hope
Snoopy's Christmas - The Mistletoe Singers
Stille Nacht - Manheim Steamroller
The Peace Carol - John Denver
The Wexford Carol - Celtic Woman
Ukranian Carol - Spencer Brewer
What Child is This - Johnny Mathis
White Christmas - Bing Crosby
White is in the Winter Night - Enya

Bonus Content:
Katarina's Taco Recipe

The Meat Filling

Flank steak is best but if you can find some other kind of beef on sale, lean but not too lean, that's fine. You'll need about 8 oz. for every person you plan to serve. That's enough for four tacos, but you know how people are – they always put in more meat than they should, so it will probably come out to more like two tacos!

Cut the meat into thin strips and mix it in a large bowl with enough lime juice, oregano, cumin, diced onions and chopped, fresh chilies to cover all the meat! Cover it and let it marinate overnight.

On the morning of taco-day, put everything into a heavy stock pot or a crock pot or a large dutch oven. Sprinkle in salt and black pepper and cook it over low heat. You want it to cook for at least eight hours, so it will be falling apart by the time you serve it! Be careful to keep the heat as low as possible so it doesn't dry out! When it's nearly done, taste it to see if it needs more salt.

The Tortillas

Normally, you don't want to make your tortillas until a few hours before the meat is done. Fresh tortillas just taste better, and are much less likely to split when overfilled. But if you're expecting a big crowd you might be better off making them ahead of time!

For every two dozen tacos, you'll need:
- 3 cups (12 ounces by weight) Masa Harina (Try to find the real thing – it really does come out better than American-style corn flour! If you don't have a tienda nearby, try looking in the international foods section of your store. Whatever you do, use corn flour, *not* cornmeal! Cornmeal just won't work!)
- 1/2 teaspoon salt
- 2 cups warm water

Mix the salt and flour together, then add the warm water and start mixing. You will need to use your hands for this! It will be too stiff for a mixer, and anyway using your hands is the only way to get your love into the food you cook! Mix it until it's all holding together like clay, but still nice and soft. If it's too sticky, dust in a little more masa. Try not to get it too dry, though, because at that point it's a real pain to add more water (but of course you can if you have to!)

Divide the dough into 24 balls of equal size (they should be about the size of golf balls – maybe just a hair bigger.)

Go ahead and start heating up your griddle, now! You want it to get about medium-hot. If you don't have a griddle you can use a large skillet. Cast iron works best - do *not* use anything "non-stick!" That stuff releases toxic gasses into the air when you heat it to the kinds of temperatures we need here!

Now squash the balls of dough one by one between your hands and then keep turning and turning them as you flatten them. If you're not too talented at that, well, some people use a rolling pin or even a tortilla press. That's OK I guess but see my comment above about the love in your hands! If you use something besides your hands, you'll need to put plastic wrap underneath and on top of the dough to keep it from sticking! Make each tortilla about four or five inches across. You don't want them bigger than that or people will put in too much filling and end up with tacos falling apart all over the place!

When you can't hold your hand a few inches above the griddle for more than half a second, it's hot enough! Throw your tortillas down on it one by one and let them cook until they're golden and bubbling a little bit on the bottom, then flip them over and cook the other side. If they puff up too high, squash them back down with a spatula!

Stack your cooked tortillas in something with a well-fitting lid as soon as you take them off the griddle. You can put them in a tortilla warmer if you have one, or a covered casserole dish, or you can just wrap them in aluminum foil.

If you have to make your tortillas more than a couple hours ahead of time, the best way to keep them fresh is to wrap stacks of them in damp towels and keep them in the refrigerator in a container

190

with a tight lid. If you do this, you'll need to warm them up before you serve them! Wrap them in foil in stacks of no more than ten per stack and tuck them into a preheated 350°F for eight to ten minutes.

The Toppings

My mother only ever put meat, chopped cilantro, and onions on her tacos! That's all I ever put on mine, too, though she diced her onions and I prefer my onions sliced very thin – I mean thin like paper! Sometimes when I'm feeling really wild I'll put on a little bit of spicy salsa, too. Don't put on too much or you'll suffer taco-in-the-lap syndrome! (I always try to tell people this but they never listen!)

But for the Vale House Christmas party I go ahead and set out lots and lots of other non-traditional toppings for the guests. What the heck – it's Christmas!

- Refried beans for vegetarian guests to choose instead of the meat filling
- Shredded cheese (if you're going to do this, at least use real Mexican queso fresco!)
- Pico de Gallo
- Mango salsa
- Tomatillo salsa verde
- Chopped chilis
- Sliced black olives
- Shredded lettuce
- Sour cream to keep the lettuce from falling off!

ABOUT THE AUTHOR

Kim Beall lives and writes in a small NC town that may or may not remind you of Woodley, USA. She has never yet met a ghost in person, though her cats do frequently manage to walk through closed doors. When not writing she gardens, hunts mushrooms, and raises chickens.

She sincerely believes every adult still yearns, not so deep inside, to find real magic in everyday life.

Other Books by Kim Beall

Seven Turns: A ~~Ghost~~ Love Story – May 2018
Moonlight and Moss – May 2019
Ghost of a Chance – May 2020
The Pizza Delivery Boy's Tale – September 2018

www.kimbeall.com
www.kimbeall.com/blog
amazon.com/author/kimbeall
goodreads.com/author/show/18012965.Kim_Beall
facebook.com/kimbeallauthor
@KimBeallsGhost